Maurice Morgann

An Essay on the Dramatic Character of Sir John Falstaff

Maurice Morgann

An Essay on the Dramatic Character of Sir John Falstaff

ISBN/EAN: 9783337303389

Printed in Europe, USA, Canada, Australia, Japan

Cover: Foto ©Andreas Hilbeck / pixelio.de

More available books at **www.hansebooks.com**

A N

E S S A Y

ON THE

DRAMATIC CHARACTER

O F

Sir *J O H N F A L S T A F F,*

I am not *John of Gaunt* your Grandfather, but yet
no COWARD, *Hal.*

First Part of HENRY IV.

L O N D O N:

PRINTED FOR T. DAVIES, IN RUSSEL-STREET,
COVENT GARDEN.

MDCCLXXVII.

PREFACE.

THE following sheets were written in confequence of a friendly converfation, turning by fome chance upon the Character of FALSTAFF, wherein the Writer, maintaining contrary to the general Opinion, that, this Character was not intended to be fhewn as a Coward, he was challenged to deliver and fupport that Opinion from the Prefs, with an engagement, now he fears forgotten, for it was three years ago, that he fhould be anfwered thro' the

fame

fame channel: Thus ftimulated, thefe papers were almoft wholly written in a very fhort time, but not without thofe attentions, whether fuccefsful or not, which feemed neceffary to carry them beyond the Prefs into the hands of the Public. From the influence of the foregoing circumftances it is, that the Writer has generally affumed rather the character and tone of an Advocate than of an Inquirer;—though if he had not firft *inquired* and been *convinced*, he fhould never have attempted to

have

have amufed either himfelf or others
with the fubject.——The impulfe of
the occafion, however, being paffed,
the papers were thrown by, and
almoft forgotten: But having been
looked into of late by fome friends,
who obferving that the Writer had
not enlarged fo far for the fake
of FALSTAFF alone, but that the
Argument was made fubfervient to
Critical amufement, perfuaded him
to revife and convey it to the
Prefs. This has been accordingly
done, though he fears fomething
too haftily, as he found it proper

to

to add, while the papers were in the courfe of printing, fome con-fiderations on the *Whole* Character of FALSTAFF; which ought to have been accompanied by a flight reform of a few preceding paffages, which may feem, in con-fequence of this addition, to con-tain too favourable a reprefentation of his Morals.

The vindication of FALSTAFF's Courage is truly no otherwife the object than fome old fantaftic Oak, or grotefque Rock, may be the object of a morning's ride ; yet being

being propofed as fuch, may ferve
to limit the diftance, and fhape
the courfe: The real object is Exercife, and the Delight which a
rich, beautiful, picturefque, and
perhaps unknown Country, may
excite from every fide. Such an
Exercife may admit of fome little
excurfion, keeping however the Road
in view; but feems to exclude
every appearance of labour and of
toil.---Under the impreffion of fuch
Feelings the Writer has endeavoured to preferve to his Text a
certain lightnefs of air, and chearfulnefs

fulnefs of tone; but is fenfible
however that the manner of difcuffion does not *every where*, particularly near the commencement,
fufficiently correfpond with his defign.---If the Book fhall be fortunate enough to obtain another Impreffion, a feparation may be made;
and fuch of the heavier parts as
cannot be wholly difpenfed with,
fink to their more proper ftation,---
a Note.

He is fearful likewife that he
may have erred in the other extreme; and that having thought
himfelf

himfelf intitled, even in argument, to a certain degree of playful dif- cuffion, may have pufhed it, in a few places, even to levity. This error might be yet more eafily re- formed than the other.—The Book is perhaps, as it ftands, too bulky for the fubject; but if the Reader knew how many preffing confide- rations, as it grew into fize, the Author refifted, which yet feemed intitled to be heard, he would the more readily excufe him.

The whole is a mere Experiment, and the Writer confiders it as fuch:

It

It may have the advantages, but it is likewife attended with all the difficulties and dangers, of *No-velty.*

ON THE

Dramatic Character

O F

Sir *JOHN FALSTAFF.*

THE ideas which I have formed concerning the Courage and Military Character of the Dramatic Sir *John Falstaff*, are so different from those which I find generally to prevail in the world, that I shall take the liberty of stating my sentiments on the subject; in hope that some person as unengaged as myself, will either correct and reform my error in this respect; or, joining himself to my opinion, redeem me from, what I may call, the reproach of singularity.

B

I am

I am to avow then, that I do not clearly difcern that Sir *John Falstaff* deferves to bear the
character fo generally given him of an abfolute
Coward; or, in other words, that I do not conceive *Shakespeare* ever meant to make Cowardice
an effential part of his conftitution.

I know how univerfally the contrary opinion
prevails; and I know what refpect and deference
are due to the public voice. But if to the avowal
of this fingularity, I add all the reafons that have
led me to it, and acknowledge myfelf to be wholly
in the judgment of the public, I fhall hope to
avoid the cenfure of too much forwardnefs or
indecorum.

It muft, in the firft place, be admitted that the
appearances in this cafe are fingularly ftrong and
ftriking; and fo they had need be, to become the
ground of fo general a cenfure. We fee this extraordinary Character, almoft in the firft moment
of our acquaintance with him, involved in circumftances

cumftances of apparent difhonour; and we hear him familiarly called *Coward* by his moft intimate companions. We fee him, on occafion of the robbery at *Gads-Hill*, in the very act of running away from the Prince and *Poins*; and we behold him, on another of more honourable obligation, in open day light, in battle, and acting in his profeffion as a Soldier, efcaping from *Douglas* even out of the world as it were; counterfeiting death, and deferting his very exiftence; and we find him on the former occafion, betrayed into thofe *lies* and *braggadocioes*, which are the ufual concomitants of Cowardice in Military men, and pretenders to valour. Thefe are not only in them-felves ftrong circumftances, but they are more-over thruft forward, preft upon our notice as the fubject of our mirth, as the great bufinefs of the fcene : No wonder, therefore, that the word fhould go forth that *Falftaff* is exhibited as a character of Cowardice and difhonour.

What there is to the contrary of this, it is my bufinefs to difcover. Much, I think, will prefently

appear;

appear; but it lies fo difperfed, is fo latent, and fo purpofely obfcured, that the reader muft have fome patience whilft I collect it into one body, and make it the object of a fteady and regular contemplation.

But what have we to do, may my readers ex-claim, with principles *fo latent, fo obfcured?* In Dramatic compofition the *Impreffion* is the *Fact*; and the Writer, who, meaning to imprefs one thing, has impreffed another, is unworthy of obfervation.

It is a very unpleafant thing to have, in the firft fetting out, fo many and fo ftrong prejudices to contend with. All that one can do in fuch cafe, is, to pray the reader to have a little pati-ence in the commencement; and to referve his cenfure, if it muft pafs, for the conclufion. Under his gracious allowance, therefore, I prefume to declare it, as my opinion, that Cowardice *is not* the *Impreffion*, which the *whole* character of *Falftaff*

is

is calculated to make on the minds of an unpre-
judiced audience ; tho' there be, I confefs, a
great deal of fomething in the *compofition* likely
enough to puzzle, and confequently to miflead
the Underftanding.—The reader will perceive
that I diftinguifh between *mental Impreffions,* and
the *Underftanding.*—I wifh to avoid every thing
that looks like fubtlety and refinement ; but this
is a diftinction, which we all comprehend.—
There are none of us unconfcious of certain feelings or fenfations of mind, which do not feem
to have paffed thro' the Underftanding ; the effects,
I fuppofe, of fome fecret influences from without,
acting upon a certain mental fenfe, and producing
feelings and paffions in juft correfpondence to
the force and variety of thofe influences on the
one hand, and to the quicknefs of our fenfibility
on the other. Be the caufe, however, what it may,
the fact is undoubtedly fo ; which is all I am
concerned in. And it is equally a fact, which
every man's experience may avouch, that the
Underftanding and thofe feelings are frequently

at

at variance. The latter often arife from the moft minute circumftances, and frequently from fuch as the Underftanding cannot eftimate, or even re- cognize ; whereas the Underftanding delights in abftraction, and in general propofitions ; which, however true confidered as fuch, are very fel- dom, I had like to have faid *never*, perfectly ap- plicable to any particular cafe. And hence, among other caufes, it is, that we often condemn or applaud characters and actions on the credit of fome logical procefs, while our hearts revolt, and would fain lead us to a very different con- clufion.

The Underftanding feems for the moft part to take cognizance of *actions* only, and from thefe to infer *motives* and *character* ; but the fenfe we have been fpeaking of proceeds in a contrary courfe ; and determines of *actions* from certain *firft principles of character*, which feem wholly out of the reach of the Underftanding. We cannot indeed do otherwife than admit that there muft

be

be diftinct principles of character in every diftinct individual : The manifeft variety even in
the minds of infants will oblige us to this. But
what *are* thefe firft principles of character?
Not the objects, I am perfuaded, of the Underftanding; and yet we take as ftrong Impreffions
of them as if we could compare and affort them
in a fyllogifm. We often love or hate at firft
fight ; and indeed, in general, diflike or approve
by fome fecret reference to thefe *principles* ; and
we judge even of conduct, not from any idea
of abftract good or evil in the nature of actions,
but by refering thofe actions to a fuppofed original
character in the man himfelf. I do not mean
that we *talk* thus; we could not indeed, if we
would, explain ourfelves in detail on this head ;
we can neither account for Impreffions and paffions, nor communicate them to others by *words:*
Tones and looks will fometimes convey the *paffion*
ftrangely, but the *Impreffion* is incommunicable.
The fame caufes may produce it indeed at the fame
time in many, but it is the feparate poffeffion of

B 4   each,

each, and not in its nature transferable: It is an imperfect fort of inftinct, and proportionably dumb.—We might indeed, if we chofe it, candidly confefs to one another, that we are greatly fwayed by thefe feelings, and are by no means fo *rational* in all points as we could wifh; but this would be a betraying of the interefts of that high faculty, the Underftanding, which we fo value ourfelves upon, and which we more peculiarly call our own. This, we think, muft not be; and fo we· huddle up the matter, concealing it as much as poffible, both from ourfelves and others. In Books indeed, wherein character, motive, and action, are all alike fubjected to the Underftanding, it is generally a very clear cafe; and we make decifions compounded of them all: And thus we are willing to approve of *Candide*, tho' he kills my Lord the Inquifitor, and runs thro' the body the Baron of *Thunder-ten-tronchk* the fon of his patron, and the brother of his beloved *Cunégonde* : But in real life, I believe, *my Lords the Judges* would be apt to inform the

Gentlemen

Gentlemen of the Jury, that my *Lord the Inquisitor*
was *ill killed*; as *Candide* did not proceed on the
urgency of the moment, but on the speculation
only of future evil. And indeed this clear per-
ception, in Novels and Plays, of the union of
character and action not seen in nature, is the
principal defect of such compositions, and what
renders them but ill pictures of human life, and
wretched guides of conduct.

But if there was *one man* in the world, who
could make a more perfect draught of real nature, and steal such Impressions on his audience,
without their special notice, as should keep their
hold in spite of any error of their Understanding,
and should thereupon venture to introduce an
apparent incongruity of character and action, for
ends which I shall presently endeavour to explain; such an imitation would be worth our
nicest curiosity and attention. But in such a case
as this, the reader might expect that he should
find us all talking the language of the Under-

standing

ftanding only ; that is, cenfuring the action with
very little confcientious inveftigation even of
that; and transferring the cenfure, in every odious colour, to the actor himfelf; how much fo-
ever our hearts and affections might fecretly
revolt : For as to the *Impreffion*, we have already
obferved that it has no tongue; nor is its
operation and influence likely to be made the
fubject of conference and communication.

It is not to the *Courage* only of *Falftaff* that we
think thefe obfervations will apply : No part
whatever of his character feems to be fully fettled
in 'our minds; at leaft there is fomething
ftrangely incongruous in our difcourfe and
affections concerning him. We all like *Old Jack*;
yet, by fome ftrange perverfe fate, we all abufe
him, and deny him the poffeffion of any one
fingle good or refpectable quality. There is
fomething extraordinary in this : It muft be a
ftrange art in *Shakefpeare* which can draw our
liking and good will towards fo offenfive an object.
He has wit, it will be faid; chearfulnefs and humour of the moft characteriftic and captivating
fort.

fort. And is this enough? Is the humour and gaiety of vice fo very captivating? Is the wit, characteriftic of bafenefs and every ill quality capable of attaching the heart and winning the affections? Or does not the apparency of fuch humour, and the flafhes of fuch wit, by more ftrongly difclofing the deformity of character, but the more effectually excite our hatred and contempt of the man? And yet this is not our *feeling* of *Falftaff*'s character. When he has ceafed to amufe us, we find no emotions of difguft; we can fcarcely forgive the ingratitude of the Prince in the new-born virtue of the King, and we curfe the feverity of that poetic juftice which configns our old good-natured delightful companion to the cuftody of the *warden*, and the difhonours of the *Fleet*.

I am willing, however, to admit that if a Dramatic writer will but preferve to any character the qualities of a ftrong mind, particularly Courage and ability, that it will be afterwards no very difficult tafk (as I may have occafion to explain)

plain) to difcharge that *difguft* which arifes from vicious manners; and even to attach us (if fuch character fhould contain any quality productive of chearfulnefs and laughter) to the caufe and fubject of our ·mirth with fome degree of affection.

But the queftion which I am to confider is of a very different nature : It is a queftion of fact, and concerning a quality which forms the bafis of every refpectable character; a quality which is the very effence of a Military man ; and which is held up to us, in almoft every Comic incident of the Play, as the fubject of our obfervation. It is ftrange then that it fhould now be a queftion, whether *Falftaff* is, or is not a man of Courage; and whether we do in fact contemn him for the want, or refpect him for the poffeffion of that quality : And yet I believe the reader will find that he has by no means decided this queftion, even. for himfelf.---If then it fhould turn out, that this difficulty has·arifen out of the Art of

Shakefpeare

Shakefpeare, who has contrived to make fecret Impreffions upon us of Courage, and to preferve thofe Impreffions in favour of a character which was to be held up for fport and laughter on account of actions of apparent Cowardice and difhonour, we fhall have lefs occafion to wonder, as *Shakefpeare* is a Name which contains All of Dramatic artifice and genius.

If in this place the reader fhall peevifhly and prematurely object that the obfervations . and diftinctions I have laboured to eftablifh, are wholly unapplicable; he being himfelf unconfcious of ever having received any fuch Impreffion; what can be done in fo nice a cafe, but to refer him to the following pages; by the number of which he may judge how very much I refpect his objection, and by the variety of thofe proofs, which I fhall employ to induce him to part with it; and to recognize in its ftead certain feelings, concealed and covered over perhaps, but not erazed, by time, reafoning, and authority.

In

In the mean while, it may not perhaps be easy for him to resolve how it comes about, that, whilst we look upon *Falstaff* as a character of the like nature with that of *Parolles* or of *Bobadil*, we should preserve for him a great degree of respect and good-will, and yet feel the highest disdain and contempt of the others, tho' they are all involved in similar situations. The reader, I believe, would wonder extremely to find either *Parolles* or *Bobadil* possess himself in danger: What then can be the cause that we are not at all surprized at the gaiety and ease of *Falstaff* un-der the most trying circumstances; and that we never think of charging *Shakespeare* with de-parting, on this account, from the truth and co-herence of character? Perhaps, after all, the *real* character of *Falstaff* may be different from his *apparent* one; and possibly this difference between reality and appearance, whilst it accounts at once for our liking and our censure, may be the true point of humour in the character, and the source of all our laughter and delight. We

may

may chance to find, if we will but examine a little into the nature of thofe circumftances which have accidentally involved him, that he was intended to be drawn as a character of much Natural courage and refolution ; and be obliged thereupon to repeal thofe decifions, which may have been made upon the credit of fome general tho' unapplicable propofitions ; the common fource of error in other and higher matters. A little reflection may perhaps bring us round again to the point of our departure, and unite our Underftandings to our inftinct.---Let us then for a moment *fufpend* at leaft our decifions, and candidly and coolly inquire if Sir *John Falftaff* be, indeed, what he has fo-often been called by critic and commentator, male and female,---a *Conftitutional Coward.*

It will fcarcely be poffible to confider the Courage of *Falftaff* as wholly detached from his other qualities : But I write not profeffedly of any part of his character, but what is included under the

term

term, *Courage*; however I may incidentally throw fome lights on the whole.---The reader will not need to be told that this Inquiry will refolve itfelf of courfe into a Critique on the ge-nius, the arts, and the conduct of *Shakefpeare*: For what is *Falftaff*, what *Lear*, what *Hamlet*, or *Othello*, but different modifications of *Shakefpeare*'s thought? It is true that this Inquiry is narrowed almoft to a fingle point: But general criticifm is as uninftructive as it is eafy: *Shakefpeare* de-ferves to be confidered in detail;---a tafk hitherto unattempted.

It may be proper, in the firft place, to take a fhort view of all the parts of *Falftaff*'s Character, and then proceed to difcover, if we can, what *Impreffions*, as to Courage or Cowardice, he had made on the perfons of the Drama: After which we will examine, in courfe, fuch evidence, either of *perfons* or *facts*, as are relative to the matter; and account as we may for thofe appearances, which feem to have led to the opinion of his Conftituti-onal Cowardice

The fcene of the robbery, and the difgraces attending it, which ftand firft in the Play, and introduce us to the knowledge of *Falftaff*, I fhall beg leave (as I think this fcene to have been the fource of much unreafonble prejudice) to *referve* till we are more fully acquainted with the whole character of *Falftaff*; and I fhall therefore hope that the reader will not for a time advert to it; or to the jefts of the *Prince* or of *Poins* in confequence of that unlucky adventure.

In drawing out the parts of *Falftaff*'s character, with which I fhall begin this Inquiry, I fhall take the liberty of putting Conftitutional bravery into his compofition ; but the reader will be pleafed to confider what I fhall fay in that refpect as fpoken hypothetically for the prefent, to be retained, or difcharged out of it, as he fhall finally determine.

To me then it appears that the leading quality in *Falftaff*'s character, and that from which all the reft take their colour, is a high degree of wit

G   and

and humour, accompanied with great natural vigour and alacrity of mind. This quality fo ac-companied, led him probably very early into life, and made him highly acceptable to fociety ; fo acceptable, as to make it feem unneceffary for him to acquire any other virtue. Hence, perhaps, his continued debaucheries and diffipations of every kind.—He feems, by nature, to have had a mind free of malice or any evil principle ; but he never took the trouble of acquiring any good one. He found himfelf efteemed and beloved with all his faults ; nay *for* his faults, which were all connected with humour, and for the moft part, grew out of it. As he had, poffibly, no vices but fuch as he thought might be openly profeffed, fo he appeared more diffolute thro' oftentation. To the character of wit and humour, to which all his other qualities feem to have conformed themfelves, he appears to have added a very ne-ceffary fupport, *that* of the profeffion of a *Soldier*. He had from nature, as I prefume to fay, a fpirit of boldnefs and enterprife ; which in a Military

age,

age, tho' employment was only occafional, kept him always above contempt, fecured him an honourable reception among the Great, and fuited beft both with his particular mode of humour and of vice. Thus living continually in fociety, nay even in Taverns, and indulging himfelf, and being indulged by others, in every debauchery; drinking, whoring, gluttony, and cafe; affuming a liberty of fiction, neceffary perhaps to his wit, and often falling into falfity and lies, he feems to have fet, by degrees, all fober reputation at defiance; and finding eternal refources in his wit, he borrows, fhifts, defrauds, and even robs, without difhonour.—Laughter and approbation attend his greateft exceffes; and being governed vifibly by no fettled bad principle or ill defign, fun and humour account for and cover all. By degrees, however, and thro' indulgence, he acquires bad habits, becomes an humourift, grows enormoufly corpulent, and falls into the infirmities of age; yet never quits, all the time, one fingle levity or vice of youth, or lofes any of that chearfulnefs of

mind,

mind, which had enabled him to pass thro' this
course with ease to himself and delight to others;
and thus, at last, mixing youth and age, enterprize and corpulency, wit and folly, poverty and
expence, title and buffoonery, innocence as to
purpose, and wickedness as to practice ; neither
incurring hatred by bad principle, or contempt
by Cowardice, yet involved in circumstances productive of imputation in both ; a butt and a wit,
a humourist and a man of humour, a touchstone
and a laughing stock, a jester and a jest, has Sir
John Falstaff, taken at that period of his life in
which we see him, become the most perfect Comic character that perhaps ever was exhibited.

It may not possibly be wholly amiss to remark
in this place, that if Sir *John Falstaff* had possessed
any of that Cardinal quality, Prudence, alike the
guardian of virtue and the protector of vice;
that quality, from the possession or the absence
of which, the character and fate of men in this
life take, I think, their colour, and not from real
vice or virtue ; if he had considered his wit not as
principal but *accessary* only ; as the instrument of
power,

power, and not as power itfelf; if he had had much
bafenefs to hide, if he had had lefs of what may
be called mellownefs or good humour, or lefs of
health and fpirit ; if he had fpurred and rode the
world with his wit, inftead of fuffering the world,
boys and all, to ride him ;---he might, without
any other effential change, have been the admi♦
ration and not the jeft of mankind :—Or if he
had lived in our day, and inftead of attaching ·
himfelf to one Prince, had renounced *all* friend♦
fhip and *all* attachment, and had let himfelf out
as the ready inftrument and Zany of every fuccef-
five Minifter, he might poffibly have acquired
the high honour of marking his fhroud or deco-
rating his coffin with the living rays of an Irifh
at leaft, if not a Britifh Coronet : Inftead of
which, tho' enforcing laughter from every difpofition, he appears, now, as fuch a character,
which every wife man will pity and avoid, every
knave will cenfure, and every fool will fear: And
accordingly *Shakefpeare*, ever true to nature, has
made *Harry* defert, and *Lancafter* cenfure him :
—He dies where he lived, in a Tavern, broken-

hearted

hearted, without a friend; and his final exit is given up to the derifion of fools. Nor has his misfortunes ended here; the fcandal arifing from the mifapplication of his wit and talents feems immortal. He has met with as little juftice or mercy from his final judges the critics, as from his companions of the Drama. With our cheeks ftill red with laughter, we ungratefully as unjuftly cenfure him as a coward by nature, and a rafcal upon principle: Tho', if this were fo, it might be hoped, for our own credit, that we fhould behold him rather with difguft and difapprobation than with pleafure and delight.

But to remember our queftion—*Is Falftaff a conftitutional coward?*

With refpect to every infirmity, except that of Cowardice, we muft take him as at the period in which he is reprefented to us. If we fee him diffipated, fat,—it is enough;—we have nothing to do with his youth, when he might perhaps have

have been modeſt, chaſte, "*and not an Eagle's talon in the waiſt*." But *Conſtitutional Courage* extends to a man's whole life, makes a part of his nature, and is not to be taken up or deſerted like a mere Moral quality. It is true, there is a Courage founded upon *principle*, or rather a principle independent of Courage, which will ſometimes operate in ſpite of nature; a principle, which prefers death to ſhame, but which always refers itſelf, in conformity to its own nature, to the prevailing modes of honour, and the faſhions of the age.---But Natural courage is another thing: It is independent of opinion; It adapts itſelf to occaſions, preſerves itſelf under every ſhape, and can avail itſelf of flight as well as of action.---In the laſt war, ſome Indians of America perceiving a line of Highlanders to keep their ſtation under every diſadvantage, and under a fire which they could not effectually return, were ſo miſerably miſtaken in our points of honour as to conjecture, from obſervation on the habit and

ſtability

ftability of thofe troops, that they were indeed
the women of England, who wanted courage to
run away.—That Courage which is founded in
nature and conftitution, *Falftaff*, as I prefume
to fay, poffeffed;—but I am ready to allow,
that the principle already mentioned, fo far as it
refers to reputation only, began with every other
Moral quality to lofe its hold on him in his old
age; that is, at the time of life in which he is
reprefented to us; a period, as it fhould feem,
approaching to *feventy*.---The truth is that he had
drollery enough to fupport himfelf in credit without the point of honour, and had addrefs enough
to make even the prefervation of his life a poinb
of drollery. The reader knows I allude, tho' fomething prematurely, to his fictitious death in the
battle of Shrewfbury. This incident is generally
conftrued to the difadvantage of *Falftaff*: It is a
tranfaction which bears the external marks of
Cowardice: It is alfo aggravated to the fpectators
by the idle tricks of the Player, who practifes

on

on this occasion all the attitudes and wild ap‑
prehensions of fear; more ambitious, as it should
seem, of reprefenting a Caliban than a *Falstaff*;
or indeed rather a poor unweildy miferable Tor‑
toife than either.---The painful Comedian lies
spread out on his belly, and not only covers him‑
felf all over with his robe as with a shell, but
forms a kind of round Tortoife-back by I know
not what stuffing or contrivance; in addition to
which, he alternately lifts up, and depresses, and
dodges his head, and looks to the one fide and to
the other, fo much with the piteous afpect of that
animal, that one would not be forry to fee the am‑
bitious imitator calipashed in his robe, and ferved
up for the entertainment of the gallery.---There
is no hint for this mummery in the Play : What‑
ever there may be of difhonour in *Falstaff*'s con‑
duct, he neither does or fays any thing on this
occafion which indicates terror or diforder of
mind : On the contrary, this very act is a
proof of his having all his wits about him, and
is a stratagem, fuch as it is, not improper for a
buffoon

buffoon, whofe fate would be fingularly hard, if he fhould not be allowed to avail himfelf of his Character when it might ferve him in moft ftead. We muft remember, in extenuation, that the executive, the deftroying hand of *Douglas* was over him : *" It was time to counterfeit, or that " hot termagant Scot had paid him scot and lot too."* He had but one choice ; he was obliged to pafs thro' the ceremony of dying either in jeft or in earneft; and we fhall not be furprized at the event, when we remember his propenfities to the former.---Life (and efpecially the life of *Falftaff*) might be a jeft ; but he could fee no joke whatever in dying : To be chopfallen was, with him, to lofe both life and character together : He faw the point of honour, as well as every thing elfe, in ridiculous lights, and began to renounce its tyranny.

But I am too much in advance, and muft retreat for more advantage. I fhould not forget how much opinion is againft me, and that I am to make my way by the mere force and

weight

weight of evidence; without which I muſt not
hope to poſſeſs myſelf of the reader : No addreſs,
no inſinuation will avail. To this evidence,
then, I now reſort. The Courage of *Falſtaff* is my
Theme: And no paſſage will I ſpare from which
any thing can be inferred as relative to this point.
It would be as vain as injudicious to attempt con-
cealment : How could I eſcape detection ? The
Play is in every one's memory, and a ſingle paſſage remembered in detection would tell, in the
mind of the partial obſerver, for fifty times its real
weight. Indeed this argument would be void of
all excuſe if it declined any difficulty; if it
did not meet, if it did not challenge oppoſition.
Every paſſage then ſhall be produced from
which, in my opinion, any inference, favourable
or unfavourable, has or can be drawn ;---but not
methodically, not formally, as texts for comment,
but as chance or convenience ſhall lead the way;
but in what ſhape ſoever, they ſhall be always
diſtinguiſhingly marked for notice. And ſo
with

with that attention to truth and candour which
ought to accompany even our lighteft amufements
I proceed to offer fuch proof as the cafe will admit, that *Courage* is a part of *Falftaff*'s *Character*,
that it belonged to his conftitution, and was manifeft in the conduct and practice of his whole
life.

Let us then examine, as a fource of very authentic information, what Impreffions *Sir John*
Falftaff had made on the characters of the Drama ;
and in what eftimation he is fuppofed to ftand
with mankind in general as to the point of Perfonal Courage. But the quotations we make for this
or other purpofes, muft, it is confeffed, be lightly
touched, and no particular paffage ftrongly re-
lied on, either in his favour or againft him.
Every thing which he himfelf fays, or is faid of
him, is fo phantaftically difcoloured by humour,
or folly, or jeft, that we muft for the moft part
look to the fpirit rather than the letter of what

is

is uttered, and rely at laſt only on a combination of the whole.

We will begin then, if the reader pleaſes, by in-quiring what Impreſſion the very Vulgar had taken of *Falſtaff*. If it is not that of Cowardice, be it what elſe it may, that of a man of violence, or *a Ruffian in years,* as Harry calls him, or any thing elſe, it anſwers my purpoſe; how inſigni-ficant ſoever the characters or incidents to be firſt produced may otherwiſe appear;---for theſe Impreſſions muſt have been taken either from perſonal knowledge and obſervation; or, what will do better for my purpoſe, from common fame. Altho' I muſt admit ſome part of this evi-dence will appear ſo weak and trifling that it certainly ought not to be produced but in proof Impreſſion only.

The *Hoſteſs Quickly* employs two officers to arreſt *Falſtaff* : On the mention of his name, one of them immediately obſerves, *"that it may chance to coſt ſome*
" of

" of them their lives, for that he will stab.--Alas a day,"
says the hostess, *" take heed of him, he cares not*
" what mischief he doth ; if his weapon be out he will
" foin like any devil; He will spare neither man,
" woman, or child." Accordingly, we find that
when they lay hold on him he resists to the utmost
of his power, and calls upon *Bardolph,* whose
arms are at liberty, to draw. *"Away, varlets, draw*
" Bardolph, cut me off the villain's head, throw the
quean in the kennel." The officers cry, *à rescue, a*
rescue ! But the Chief Justice comes in and the
scuffle ceases. In another scene, his wench *Doll*
Tearsheet asks him *" when he will leave fighting*
* * * * * *and patch up his old body for heaven."*
This is occasioned by his drawing his rapier, on
great provocation, and driving *Pistol,* who is
drawn likewise, down stairs, and hurting him in
the shoulder. To drive *Pistol* was no great feat;
nor do I mention it as such; but upon this
occasion it was necessary. *"A Rascal bragging slave,*
says he, *" the rogue fled from me like quickfilver."* Ex-
preffions, which as they remember the cow-

ardice

ardice of *Piſtol*, ſeem to prove that *Falſtaff* did not value himſelf on the adventure. Even ſomething may be drawn from *Davy, Shallow's* ſerving man, who calls *Falſtaff*, in ignorant admiration, the *man of war*. I muſt obſerve here, and I beg the reader will notice it, that there is not a ſingle expreſſion dropt by theſe people, or either of *Falſtaff's* followers, from which may be inferred the leaſt ſuſpicion of Cowardice in his character; and this is I think ſuch an *implied negation* as deſerves conſiderable weight.

But to go a little higher, if, indeed, to conſider *Shallow's* opinion be to go *higher* : It is from him, however, that we get the earlieſt account of Falſtaff. He *remembers him a Page to Thomas Mowbray Duke of Norfolk* : *"He broke,* ſays he, *"Schoggan's head at the Court-Gate when he was " but a crack thus high."* *Shallow*, throughout, conſiders him as a great Leader and Soldier, and relates this fact as an early indication only of his future Prowefs. *Shallow* it is true, is a very ridiculous

culous character; but he picked up thefe Impreffions fomewhere; and he picked up none of
a contrary tendency.—I want at prefent only to
prove that *Falftaff* ftood well in the report of common fame as to this point; and he was now near
feventy years of age, and had paffed in a Military
line thro' the active part of his life. At this
period common fame may be well confidered as
the *feal* of his character; a feal which ought not
perhaps to be broke open on the evidence of any
future tranfaction.

But to proceed. *Lord Bardolph* was a man of
the world, and of fenfe and obfervation. He informs *Northumberland*, erroneoufly indeed, that
Percy had beaten the King at Shrewfbury. "*The
King*," according to him, " *was wounded; the
" Prince of Wales and the two Blunts flain, certain
" Nobles,* whom he names, *had efcaped by flight, and
" the Brawn Sir John Falftaff was taken prifoner.* "
But how came *Falftaff* into this lift? Common
fame had put him there. He is fingularly obliged

ged to Common fame.---But if he had not been
a Soldier of repute, if he had not been brave as
well as fat; if he had been *mere brawn*, it would
have been more germane to the matter if this
lord had put him down among the baggage or
the provender. The fact seems to be; that there
is a real confequence about Sir *John Falſtaff* which
is not brought forward ! We fee him only in his
familiar hours; we enter the tavern with *Hal*
and *Poins*; we join in the laugh and *take a pride
to gird at him* : But there may be a great deal of
truth in what he himſelf writes to the Prince; that
that tho' he be "*Jack Falſtaff with his Familiars, he
is* Sir John *with the reſt of Europe*:" It has been re-
marked, and very truly I believe, that no man is
a hero in the eye of his valet-de-chambre; and
thus it is, we are witneſſes only of *Falſtaff's* weak-
neſs and buffoonery;-our acquaintance is with
Jack Falſtaff, Plump Jack; and *Sir John Paunch*; but
if we would look for *Sir John Falſtaff*, we muſt put
on, as *Bunyan* would have expreſſed it, the ſpecta-
cles of obſervation. With reſpect, for inſtance,

D   to

to his Military command at Shrewſbury, nothing appears on the ſurface but the Prince's familiarly ſaying, in the tone uſually aſſumed when ſpeaking of *Falſtaff*, "*I will procure this fat rogue a Charge* " *of foot* ; " and in another place, " *I will procure* " *thee Jack a Charge of foot* ; *meet me to-morrow in the* " *Temple Hall.*" Indeed we might venture to infer from this, that a Prince of ſo great ability, whoſe wildneſs was only external and aſſumed, would not have procured, in ſo nice and critical a conjuncture, a Charge of foot for a known Coward. But there was more it ſeems in the caſe : We now find from this report, to which *Lord Bardolph* had given full credit, that the world had its eye upon *Falſtaff* as an officer of merit, whom it expected to find in the field, and whoſe fate in the battle was an object of Public concern : His life was, it ſeems, very material indeed ; a thread of ſo much dependence, that *fiction*, weaving the fates of Princes, did not think it unworthy, how coarſe ſoever, of being made a part of the tiſſue.

We

We fhall next produce the evidence of the Chief Juftice of England. He inquires of his attendant, " *if the man who was then paffing him was* " *Falftaff; he who was in queftion for the robbery.*" The attendant anfwers affirmatively, but reminds his lord " *that he had fince done good fervice at Shrewfbury;* " and the Chief Juftice, on this occafion, rating him for his debaucheries, tells him " *that his day's fervice at Shrewfbury had gilded over* " *his night's exploit at Gads Hill.*" This is furely more than Common fame : *The Chief Juftice* muft have known his whole character taken together, and muft have received the moft authentic information, and in the trueft colours, of his behaviour in that action.

But, perhaps, after all, the Military men may be efteemed the beft judges in points of this nature. Let us hear then *Coleville* of the dale, *a Soldier, in degree a Knight, a famous rebel, and* " *whofe* " *betters, had they been ruled by him, would have fold* " *themfelves dearer :*" A man who is of confequence

enough

enough to be gaurded by *Blunt* and *led to prefent execution.* This man yields himfelf up even to the very Name and Reputation of *Falftaff.* " *I think,* " fays he, "*you are Sir John Falftaff, and in that thought* " *yield me.* " But this is but one only among the men of the fword; they fhall be produced then by *dozens,* if that will fatisfy. Upon the return of the King and Prince Henry from Wales, the Prince feeks out and finds *Falftaff* debauching in a tavern ; where *Peto* prefently brings an account of ill news from thé North ; and adds, " *that as he came along he met or overtook a dozen Captains, bare headed, fweating, knocking at the taverns, aud afking every one for* Sir John Falftaff. He is followed by *Bardolph,* who informs *Falftaff* that "*He muft away* " *to the Court immediately* ; *a dozen Captains ftay at* " *door for him.*" Hére is Military evidence in abund-ance, and *Court evidence* too ; for what are we to infer from *Falftaff*'s being fent for to Court ori this ill news, but that his opinion was to be afked, as a Military man of fkill and experience, concern-ing the defences neceffary to be taken. Nor is

Shakefpear

Shakespeare content, here, with leaving us to gather up *Falstaff's better character* from inference and deduction : He comments on the fact by making *Falstaff* obferve that " *Men of merit are fought after :* " *The undeferver may fleep when the man of action is* " *called on.* " I do not wifh to draw *Falstaff's* character out of his own mouth ; but this obfervation refers to the fact, and is founded in reafon. Nor ought we to reject, what in another place he fays to the Chief Juftice, as it is in the nature of an appeal to his knowledge. " *There is not a dan-* " *gerous action,* " fays he, " *can peep out his head but* *I am thruft upon it.* " The Chief Juftice feems by his anfwer to admit the fact. " *Well, be honeft, be* *honeft, and heaven blefs your expedition.* " But the whole paffage may deferve tranfcribing.

Ch. Juft. " *Well, the King has fevered you and* *Prince Henry. I hear you are going with Lord John* *of Lancafter, againft the Archbifhop and the Earl of* *Northumberland.* "

D 3

" Falf.

" Falſ. *Yes, I thank your pretty ſweet wit for it; but*
" *look you pray, all you that kiſs my lady peace at home,*
" *that our armies join not in a hot day; for I take but*
" *two ſhirts out with me, and I mean not to ſweat ex-*
" *traordinarily : If it be a hot day, if I brandiſh any*
" *thing but a bottle, would I might never ſpit white*
" *again. There is not a dangerous action can peep*
" *'out his head but I am thruſt upon it. Well I cannot*
" *laſt for ever.---But it was always the trick of our*
" *Engliſh nation, if they have a good thing to make it*
" *too common. If you will needs ſay I am an old man*
" *you ſhould give me reſt : I would to God my name*
" *were not ſo terrible to the enemy as it is. I were*
" *better to be eaten to death with a ruſt than to be ſcour'd*
" *to nothing with perpetual motion.*"

" Ch. Juſt. *Well be honeſt, be honeſt, and heaven*
" *bleſs your expedition.*"

Falſtaff indulges himſelf here in humourous
exaggeration ;---theſe paſſages are not meant to
be taken, nor are we to ſuppoſe that they were
taken

taken, literally ;---but if there was not a ground
of truth, if *Falſtaff* had not had ſuch a degree of
Military reputation as was capable of being thus
humorouſly amplified and exaggerated, the
whole dialogue would have been highly prepoſterous and abſurd, and the acquieſcing anſwer of
the *Lord Chief Juſtice* ſingularly improper.---But
upon the ſuppoſition of *Falſtaff's* being conſidered, upon the whole, as a good and gallant Officer,
the anſwer is juſt, and correſponds with the acknowledgment which had a little before been
made, "*that his day's ſervice at Shrewſbury had gilded*
"*over his night's exploit at Gads Hill.---You may*
"*thank the unquiet time*, ſays the Chief Juſtice,
"*for your quiet o'erpoſting of that action ;*" agreeing
with what *Falſtaff* ſays in another place ;---"*Well*
"*God be thanked for theſe Rebels, they offend none but*
"*the virtuous; I laud them, I praiſe them.*"---Whe-
ther this be ſaid in the true ſpirit of a Soldier or
not, I do not determine ; it is ſurely not in that
of a mere Coward and Poltroon.

It

It will be needlefs to fhew, which might be
done from a variety of particulars, that *Falftaff*
was known, and had confideration at Court. *Shallow* cultivates him in the idea that *a friend at Court
is better than a penny in purfe:* *Weftmorland*
fpeaks to him in the tone of an equal : Upon
Falftaff's telling him, that he thought his lord-
fhip had been already at Shrewfbury, *Weftmorland* replies,---*Faith Sir John, 'tis more than time
" that I were there, and you too ; the King I can tell
" you looks for us all; we muft away all to night.---
" Tut, fays Falftaff, never fear me, I am as vigilant
" as a cat to fteal cream."---He defires, in another
place, of my lord John of Lancafter, " that when
he goes to Court, he may ftand in his good report."*
His intercourfe and correfpondence with both
thefe lords feem eafy and familiar. *Go,* fays he to
the page, *"bear this to my Lord of Lancafter, this
" to the Prince, this to the Earl of Weftmorland, and
" this* (for he extended himfelf on all fides) *to
old Mrs. Urfula,"* whom it feems, the rogue ought
to have married many years before.---But thefe
intimations

intimations are needlefs : We fee him ourfelves in
the *Royal Prefence*; where, certainly, his buffooneries
never brought him; nor was the Prince of a character to commit fo high an indecorum, as to
thruft, upon a folemn occafion, a mere Tavern
companion into his father's Prefence, efpecially
in a moment when he himfelf deferts his loofer
character, and takes up that of *a Prince indeed.*
—In a very important fcene, where *Worcefter* is
expected with propofals from *Percy,* and wherein he is received, is treated with, and carries
back offers of accomodation from the King,
the King's attendants upon the occafion are
*the Prince of Wales, Lord John of Lancafter, the
Earl of Weftmorland, Sir Walter Blunt, and Sir John
Falftaff.*—What fhall be faid to this? Falftaff is
not furely introduced here in vicious indulgence
to a mob audience ;—he utters but one word,
a buffoon one indeed, but afide and to the Prince
only. Nothing, it fhould feem, is wanting, if
decorum would here have permitted, but that
he fhould have fpoken one fober fentence in the

Prefence

Prefence (which yet we are to fuppofe him ready
and able to do if occafion fhould have required ;
or his wit was given him to little purpofe) and
Sir *John Falftaff* might be allowed to pafs for an
eftablifhed Courtier and counfellor of ftate. " *If*
" *I do grow great,* fays he, *I'll grow lefs, purge and*
" *leave fack, and live as a nobleman fhould do.*" Nobility did not then appear to him at an unmea-
furable diftance ; it was, it feems, in his idea,
the very next link in the chain.

But to return. I would now demand what could
bring *Falftaff* into the Royal Prefence upon fuch
an occafion, or juftify the Prince's fo public acknowledgment of him, but an eftablifhed fame
and reputation of Military merit ? In fhort, juft
the like merit as brought Sir *Walter Blunt* into
the fame circumftances of honour.

But it may be objected that his introduction
into this fcene is a piece of indecorum in the
author. But upon what ground are we to fuppofe

pofe this ? Upon the ground of his being a no-
torious Coward ? Why this is the very point in
queftion, and cannot be granted : Even the direct
contrary I have affirmed, and am endeavouring
to fupport. But if it be fuppofed upon any other
ground, it does not concern me; I have nothing
to do with *Shakefpeare*'s indecorums in general.
That there are indecorums in the Play I have no
doubt : The indecent treatment of *Percy*'s dead
body is the greateft ;---the familiarity of the infig-
nificant, rude, and even ill difpofed *Poins* with the
Prince, is another ;-- but the admiffion of *Falftaff*
into the Royal Prefence (fuppofing, which I have
a right to fuppofe, that his Military character
was unimpeached) does not feem to be in any
refpect among the number. In camps there is
but one virtue and one vice ; Military merit
fwallows up or covers all. But, after all, what
have we do with indecorums ? Indecorums refpect the propriety or impropriety of exhibiting
certain actions ;---not their *truth* or *falfhood* when
exhibited. *Shakefpeare* ftands to us in the place
of

of *truth* and *nature* : If we defert this principle
we cut the turf from under us ; I may then object to the robbery and other paffages as indecorums, and as contrary to the truth of character.
In fhort we may rend and tear the Play to pieces,
and every man carry off what fentences he likes
beft.--But why this inveterate malice againft poor
Falftaff ? He has faults enough in confcience without loading him with the infamy of Cowardice; a
charge, which, if true, would, if I am not greatly miftaken, fpoil all our mirth,---But of that
hereafter.

It feems to me that, in our hafty judgment of
fome particular tranfactions, we forget the circumftances and condition of his whole life and
character, which yet deferve our very particular
attention.   The author, it is true, has thrown the
moft advantageous of thefe circumftances into the
back ground as it were, and has brought nothing
out of the canvafs but his follies and buffoonery.
We difcover however, that in a very early period
of

of his life he was familiar with *John* of *Gaunt*;
which could hardly be, unlefs he had poffeffed
much perfonal gallantry and accomplifhment, and
had derived his birth from a diftinguifhed at
leaft, if not from a Noble family.

It may feem very extravagant to infift upon
Falftaff's birth as a ground from which, by any
inference, Perfonal courage may be derived,
efpecially after having acknowledged that he
feemed to have deferted thofe points of honour,
which are more peculiarly the accompanyments
of rank. But it may be obferved that in the
Feudal ages rank and wealth were not only connected with the point of honour, but with perfonal ftrength and natural courage. It is obferv-
able that Courage is a quality, which is at leaft
as tranfmiffible to one's pofterity as features and
complexion. In thefe periods men acquired and
maintained their rank and poffeffions by perfonal
prowefs and gallantry; and their marriage alli-
ances were made, of courfe, in families of the
fame

fame character : And from hence, and from the
exercifes of their youth, we muft account for the
diftinguifhed force and bravery of our antient
Barons. It is not therefore befide my purpofe
to inquire what hints of the origin and birth of
Falftaff, Shakefpeare may have dropped in different
parts of the Play ; for tho' we may be difpofed
to allow that *Falftaff* in his old age might, under
particular influences, defert the point of honour,
we cannot give up that unalienable poffeffion
of Courage, which might have been derived to
him from a noble or diftinguifhed ftock.

But it may be faid that *Falftaff* was in truth the
child of invention only, and that a reference to
the Feudal accidents of birth ferves only to confound fiction with reality : Not altogether fo.
If the ideas of Courage and *birth* were ftrongly
affociated in the days of *Shakefpeare*, then would
the affignment of high birth to *Falftaff* carry, and
be intended to carry along with it, to the minds
of the audience the affociated idea of Courage,

if

if nothing should be specially interpofed to dif-
folve the connection;—and the question is as
concerning this intention, and this effect.

I shall proceed yet farther to make a few very
minute obfervations of the fame nature: But
if *Shakefpeare* meant fometimes rather to *imprefs*
than explain, no circumftances calculated to this
end, either directly or by affociation, are too minute
for notice. But however this may be, a more con-
ciliating reafon ftill remains: The argument itfelf, like the tales of our Novelifts, is a *vehicle*
only ; *theirs*, as they profefs, of moral inftruction;
and *mine* of critical amufement. The vindication
of *Falftaff*'s Courage deferves not for its own fake
the leaft fober difcuffion ; *Falftaff* is the word only,
Shakefpeare is the *Theme*: And if thro' this channel, I can furnifh no irrational amufement, the
reader will not, perhaps, every where expect from
me the ftrict feverity of logical inveftigation.

Falftaff, then, it may be obferved, was introduced into the world,--- (at leaft we are told fo)
by

by the name of *Oldcaſtle*.* This was aſſigning
him an origin of nobility ; but the family of that
name diſclaiming any kindred with his vices, he
was thereupon, as it is ſaid, ingrafted into another ſtock† ſcarcely leſs diſtinguiſhed, tho' fallen into indelible diſgraces ; and by this means

* I believe the ſtage was in poſſeſſion of ſome rude
outline of *Falſtaff* before the time of *Shakeſpeare*, under
the name of *Sir John Oldcaſtle* ; and I think it probable
that this name was retained for a period in *Shakeſpeare's*
Hen. 4th. but changed to *Falſtaff* before the play was
printed. The expreſſion of " *Old Lad of the Caſtle*,"
uſed by the Prince, does not however decidedly
prove this ; as it might have been only ſome known
and familiar appellation too careleſly transferred from
the old Play.

† I doubt if *Shakeſpeare* had Sir *John Faſtolfe* in
his memory when he called the character under conſideration *Falſtaff*. The title and name of *Sir John*
were transferred from *Oldcaſtle* not *Faſtolfe*, and there
is no kind of ſimilarity in the characters. If he had
Faſtolfe in his thought at all, it was that while he ap-
proached the name, he might make ſuch a departure
from it as the difference of character ſeemed to
require.

he

he has been made, if the conjectures of certain
critics are well founded, the Dramatic fucceffor,
tho', having refpect to chronology, the natural
proavus of another Sir *John,* who was no lefs than
a Knight of the moft noble order of the Garter,
but a name for ever difhonoured by a frequent
expofure in that Drum-and-trumpet Thing called *The firft part of Henry* VI. written doubtlefs,
or rather exhibited, long before *Shakefpeare* was
born, * tho' afterwards repaired, I think, and

E   furbifhed

---

* It would be no difficult matter I think to prove
that all thofe Plays taken from the Englifh chronicle,
which are afcribed to *Shakefpeare,* were on the ftage
before his time, and that he was employed by the Players only to refit and repair ; taking due care to retain
the names of the characters and to preferve all thofe
incidents which were the moft popular. Some of thefe
Plays, particularly the two parts of Hen. IV. have,
certainly received what may be called a *thorough repair* ;
that is, *Shakefpeare* new-wrote them to the old names.
In the latter part of Hen. V. fome of the old materials remain ; and in the Play which I have here cenfured (Hen. VI.) we fee very little of the new. I fhould
conceive it would not be very difficult to feel one's

way

furbiſhed up by him with here and there a little
ſentiment and diction.   This family, if any

branch

way thro' theſe Plays, and diſtinguiſh every where
the metal from the clay.   Of the two Plays of Hen.
IV.ᵗ. there has been, I have admitted, a complete
tranſmutation, preſerving the old forms; but in the
others, there is often no union or coaleſcence of parts, nor
are any of them equal in merit to thoſe Plays more peculiarly and emphatically *Shakeſpeare's own.* The reader
will be pleaſed to think that I do not reckon into the
works of *Shakeſpeare* certain abſurd productions which
his editors have been ſo good as to compliment him
with.   I object, and ſtrenuouſly too, even to *The Tam-
ing of the Shrew;* not that it wants merit, but that it
does not bear the peculiar features and ſtamp of
Shakeſpeare.

   The rhyming parts of the Hiſtoric plays are all, I
think, of an older date than the times of *Shakeſpeare.*
--There was a Play, I believe, of *the Acts of King John,*
of which the baſtard *Falconbridge* ſeems to have been
the hero and the fool : He appears to have ſpoken altogether in rhyme.   *Shakeſp.are* ſhews him to us in the
latter part of the ſecond ſcene in the firſt act of *King
John* in this condition; tho' he afterwards, in the courſe
of the Play, thought fit to adopt him, to give him language and manners, and to make him his own.

branch of it remained in *Shakefpeare's* time,
might have been proud of their Dramatic ally,
if indeed they could have any fair pretence to
claim as fuch *him* whom *Shakefpeare*, perhaps in
contempt of Cowardice, wrote *Falftaff*, not *Faftolfe*,
the true Hiftoric name of the Gartered Craven.

In the age of Henry IV. a Family creft and
arms were authentic proofs of gentility ; and this-
proof, among others, *Shakefpeare* has furnifhed us
with : *Falftaff* always carried about him, it feems,
a Seal ring of his Grandfather's worth, as he fays,
forty marks : The Prince indeed affirms, but not
ferioufly I think, that this ring was *copper.* As
to the exiftence of the *bonds,* which were I fuppofe the negotiable fecurities or paper money of
the time, and which he pretended to have loft,
I have nothing to fay ; but the ring, I believe,
was really gold ; tho' probably a little too much
alloyed with bafer metal. But this is not the
point : The *arms* were doubtlefs genuine ; they
were borne by his Grandfather, and are proofs
of an antient gentility ; a gentility doubtlefs, in

former

former periods, connected with wealth and poffeffions, tho' the gold of the family might have
been tranfmuting by degrees, and perhaps, in the
hands of *Falftaff*, converted into little better than
copper. This obfervation is made on the fuppofition of *Falftaff*'s being confidered as the head
of the family, which I think however he ought
not to be. It appears rather as if he ought to
be taken in the light of a cadet or younger brother; which the familiar appellation of *John*,
" the only one (as he fays) given him by his bro-
" thers and fifters," feems to indicate. Be this
as it may, we find he is able, in fpite of diffipation,
to keep up a certain *ftate* and *dignity* of appearance;
retaining no lefs than four, if not five, followers
or men fervants in his train. He appears alfo
to have had apartments in town, and, by his in-
vitations of *Mafter Gower* to dinner and to fupper,
a regular table: And one may infer farther from
the Prince's queftion, on his return from Wales,
to *Bardolph*, " *Is your mafter* here *in London*," that
he had likewife a houfe in the country. Slight

proofs

proofs it muſt be confeſſed, yet the inferences are ſo probable, ſo buoyant, in their own nature, that they may well reſt on them, That he did not lodge at the Tavern is clear from the circumſtances of the arreſt. Theſe various occaſions of expence,---ſervants, taverns, houſes, and and whores,---neceſſarily imply that *Falſtaff* muſt have had ſome funds which are not brought immediately under our notice. That theſe funds were not however adequate to his ſtyle of living is plain: Perhaps his train may be conſidered only as incumbrances, which the pride of family and the habit of former opulence might have brought upon his preſent poverty: I do not mean abſolute poverty, but call it ſo as relative to his expence. To have *" but ſeven groats " and two-pence in his purſe "* and a page to bear it, is truly ridiculous; and it is for that reaſon we become ſo familiar with its contents, *"He " can find"* he ſays, *" no remedy for this conſumption " of the purſe, borrowing does but linger and linger " it out; but the diſeaſe is incurable. "* It might well be deemed ſo in his courſe of diſſipation: But I

E 3   ſhall fhall prefently fuggeft one fource at leaft of his fupply much more conftant and honourable than that of borrowing. But the condition of *Falftaff* as to opulence or poverty is not very material to my purpofe : It is enough if his birth was diftinguifhéd, and his youth noted for gallantry and accomplifhments. To the firft I have fpoken, and as for the latter we fhall not be at a lofs when we remember that " *he was in his youth a page to Thomas Mowbray Duke of Norfolk*;" a fituation at that time fought for by young men of the beft families and firft fortune. The houfe of every great noble was at that period a kind of Military fchool; and it is probable that *Falftaff* was fingularly adroit at his exercifes: " *He broke Schoggan's* " *head,* " (fome boifterous fencer I fuppofe) " *when he was but a crack thus high,* " *Shallow* remembers him *as notedly fkilful at backfword*; and he was at that period, according to his own humourous account, "*fcarcely an eagle's talon in the waift, and could have crept thro' an alderman's thumb* " *ring.* " Even at the age at which he is exibited to us, we find him *foundering*, as he calls it, *nine score and odd miles*, with wonderful expedition, to join the army of Prince John of Lancaſter ; and declaring after the ſurrender of *Coleville*, that " *had he but a belly of any indifferency he were ſimply* " *the moſt active fellow in Europe.*" Nor ought we here to paſs over his Knighthood without notice. It was, I grant, intended by the author as a dig-nity which, like his Courage and his wit, was to be debaſed ; his knighthood by low ſituations, his Courage by circumſtances and imputations of cowardice, and his wit by buffoonery. But how are we to ſuppoſe this honour was acquired ? By that very Courage, it ſhould ſeem, which we ſo obſtinately deny him. It was not certainly given him, like a modern City Knighthood, for his wealth or gravity : It was in theſe days a Military ho-nour, and an authentic badge of Military merit.

But *Falſtaff* was not only a Military Knight, he poſſeſs'd an honourable *penſion* into the bargain ; the reward as well as retainer of ſervice, and which ſeems (beſides the favours per-

haps

haps of Mrs. *Urfula*) to be the principal and only, folid fupport of his prefent expences. But let us refer to the paffage. "*A pox of this gout, or a gout* "*of this pox ; for one or the other plays the rogue with* "*my great toe :* *It is no matter if I do halt, I have the* "*wars for my colour and my penfion fhall feem the more* "*reafonable.*" The mention *Falftaff* here makes of a penfion, has I believe been generally con-ftrued to refer rather to *hope* than *poffeffion*, yet I know not why : For the poffeffive MY, *my penfion* (not *a* penfion) requires a different conftruction. Is it that we cannot enjoy a wit, till we have ftript him of every worldly advantage, and redu-ced him below the level of our envy ? It may be perhaps for this reafon among others that *Shake-fpeare* has fo obfcured the better parts of *Falftaff* and ftolen them fecretly on our feelings, inftead of opening them fairly to the notice of our un-derftandings. How carelefly, and thro' what bye-paths, as it were, of cafual inference is this fact of a penfion introduced ! And how has he affociated it with misfortune and infirmity ! Yet

I queftion

I queſtion, however, if, in this one place the *Impreſſion* which was intended, be well and effec-tually made. It muſt be left to the reader to de-termine if in that maſs of things out of which *Falſtaff* is compounded, he ever conſidered a penſion as any part of the compoſition : A pen-ſion however he appears to have had, one that halting could only ſeem to make more reaſon-able, not more honourable. The inference ari-ſing from the faɛt, I ſhall leave to the reader. It is ſurely a circumſtance highly advantageous to *Falſtaff*, (I ſpeak of the penſions of former days) whether he be conſidered in the light of a ſoldier or a gentleman.

I cannot foreſee the temper of the reader, nor whether he be content to go along with me in theſe kind of obſervations. Some of the inci-dents which I have drawn out of the Play may appear too minute, whilſt yet they refer to prin-ciples, which may ſeem too general. Many points require explanation ; ſomething ſhould be ſaid of the nature of *Shakeſpeare*'s Dramatic cha-racters ;

racters; * by what arts they were formed, and
wherein they differ from thofe of other writers;
fomething likewife more profeffedly of *Shake-*
fpeare

* The reader muft be fenfible of fomething in the
compofition of *Shakefpeare*'s characters, which renders
them effentially different from thofe drawn by other
writers. The characters of every Drama muft indeed
be grouped ; but in the groupes of other poets the
parts which are not feen, do not in fact exift. But
there is a certain roundnefs and integrity in the forms
of *Shakefpeare,* which give them an independence as
well as a relation, infomuch that we often meet with
paffages, which tho' perfectly felt, cannot be fufficiently explained in words, without unfolding the
whole character of the fpeaker : And this I may be
obliged to do in refpect to that of *Lancafter,* in order
to account for fome words fpoken by him in cenfure
of *Falftaff.*---Something which may be thought too
heavy for the *text,* I fhall add *here,* as a conjecture concerning the compofition of *Shakefpeare*'s characters : Not
that they were the effect, I believe, fo much of a minute
and laborious attention, as of a certain comprehenfive
energy of mind, involving within itfelf all the effects
of fyftem and of labour.

Bodies

fpeare himfelf, and of the peculiar character of his genius. After fuch a review we may not perhaps think any confideration arifing out of the

Bodies of all kinds, whether of metals, plants, or animals, are fuppofed to poffefs certain firft principles of *being*, and to have an exiftence independent of the accidents, which form their magnitude or growth : Thofe accidents are fuppofed to be drawn in from the furrounding elements, but not indifcriminately ; each plant and each animal, imbibes thofe things only, which are proper to its own diftinct nature, and which have befides fuch a fecret relation to each other as to be capable of forming a perfect union and coalefcence : But fo varioufly are the furrounding elements mingled and difpofed, that each particular body, even of thofe under the fame fpecies, has yet fome *peculiar* of its own. *Shakefpeare* appears to have confidered the being and growth of the human mind as analagous to this fyftem : There are certain qualities and capacities, which he feems to have confidered as firft principles ; the chief of which are certain energies of courage and activity, according to their degrees; together with different degrees and forts of fenfibilities, and a capacity, varying likewife in the *degree*, of difcernment and intelligence. The reft of the compofition

the Play, or out of general nature, either as too
minute or too extenfive.

Shakefpeare is in truth, an author whofe mimic
creation agrees in general fo perfectly with that

of

tion is drawn in from an atmofphere of furrounding
things; that is, from the various influences of the different laws, religions and governments in the world; and
from thofe of the different ranks and inequalities in
fociety; and from the different profeffions of men, encouraging or repreffing paffions of particular forts, and
inducing different modes of thinking and habits of life;
and he feems to have known intuitively what thofe
influences in particular were which this or that origi-
ginal conftitution would moft freely imbibe, and which
would moft eafily affociate and coalefce. But all thefe
things being, in different fituations, very differently
difpofed, and thofe differences exactly difcerned by
him, he found no difficulty in marking every individual, even among characters of the fame fort, with
fomething peculiar and diftinct.---Climate and complexion demand their influence, " Be thus when thou
art dead, and I will kill thee, and love thee after,"
is a fentiment characteriftic of, and fit only to be uttered
by a Moor.

But

of nature, that it is not only wonderful in the
great, but opens another scene of amazement to the
difcoveries of the microfcope. We have been char-
ged indeed by a Foreign writer with an overmuch
admiring of this *Barbarian* : Whether we have
admired

But it was not enough for *Shakefpeare* to have formed
his characters with the moft perfect truth and coherence ; it was further neceffary that he fhould poffefs
a wonderful facility of compreffing, as it were, his
own fpirit into thefe images, and of giving alternate
animation to the forms. This was not to be done
from without ; he muft have *felt* every varied fituation, and have fpoken thro' the organ he had formed. Such an intuitive comprehenfion of things and
fuch a facility, muft unite to produce a *Shakefpeare.*
The reader will not now be furprifed if I affirm that
thofe characters in *Shakefpeare,* which are feen only in
part, are yet capable of being unfolded and underftood
in the whole ; every part being in fact relative, and
inferring all the reft. It is true that the point of action
or fentiment, which we are moft concerned in, is always held out for our fpecial notice. But who does
not perceive that there is a peculiarity about it, which
conveys a relifh of the whole ? And very frequently,
when

admired with knowledge, or have blindly followed thofe feelings of affection which we could
not refift, I cannot tell ; but certain it is, that to
the labours of his Editors he has not been overmuch obliged. They are however for the moft
part of the firft rank in literary fame ; but fome

of

when no particular point preffes, he boldly makes a
character act and fpeak from thofe parts of the compofition, which are *inferred* only, and not diftinctly
fhewn. This produces a wonderful effect ; it feems
to carry us beyond the poet to nature itfelf, and gives
an integrity and truth to facts and character, which
they could not otherwife obtain : And this is in reality that art in *Shakefpeare*, which being withdrawn
from our notice, we more emphatically call *nature*.
A felt propriety and truth from caufes unfeen, I take
to be the higheft point of Poetic compofition. If the
characters of *Shakefpeare* are thus *whole*, and as it were
original, while thofe of almoft all others writers are
mere imitation, it may be fit to confider them rather
as Hiftoric than Dramatic beings ; and, when occafion
requires, to account for their conduct from the *whole*
of character, from general principles, from latent motives, and from policies not avowed.

of them had poffeffions of their own in Parnaf-
fus, of an extent too great and important to allow of a very diligent attention to the interefts
of others; and among thofe Critics more
profeffionally fo, the ableft and the beft has unfortunately looked more to the praife of inge-
nious than of juft conjecture. The character of
his emendations are not fo much that of *right*
or *wrong*, as that, being in the extreme, they
are always *Warburtonian*. Another has fince
undertaken the cuftody of our author, whom he
feems to confider as a fort of wild Proteus or madman, and accordingly knocks him down with the
butt-end of his critical ftaff, as often as he ex-
ceeds that line of fober difcretion, which this
learned Editor appears to have chalked out for
him : Yet is this Editor notwithftanding " a man
take him for all in all, " very highly refpectable for his genius and his learning. What
however may be chiefly complained of in thefe
gentlemen is, that having erected themfelves
into the condition, as it were, of guardians and

truftees

truftees of *Shakefpeare*; they have never undertaken to difcharge the difgraceful incumbrances of fome wretched productions, which have
long hung heavy on his fame.   Befides the evidence of tafte,' which indeed is not communica-
ble,   there   are   yet   other   and   more general
proofs that thefe incumbrances were not incurred by *Shakefpeare :* The *Latin* fentences difperfed thro' the imputed trafh is, I think, of itfelf
a decifive one. *Love's Labour loft* contains a
very conclufive one of another kind ; tho' the
very laft Editor has, I believe, in his critical
fagacity, fupprefled the evidence, and withdrawn
the record.

Yet whatever may be the neglect of fome, or
the cenfure of others, there are thofe, who firmly
believe that this wild, this uncultivated Barbarian, has not yet obtained one half of his fame ;
and who truft that fome new Stagyrite will arife,
who inftead of pecking at the furface of things
will enter into the inward foul of his compofi-
tions, and expel by the force of congenial
feelings

feelings, thofe foreign impurities which have ftained and difgraced his page. And as to thofe *fpots* which will ftill remain; they may perhaps become invifible to thofe who fhall feek them thro' the medium of his beauties, inftead of looking for thofe beauties; as is too frequently done, thro' the fmoke of fome real or imputed obfcurity. When the hand of time fhall have brufhed off his prefent Editors and Commentators, and when the very name of *Voltaire*, and even the memory of the language in which he has written, fhall be no more, the *Apalachian* mountains, the banks of the *Ohio*, and the plains of *Sciota* fhall refound with the accents of this Barbarian: In his native tongue he fhall roll the genuine paffions of nature; nor fhall the griefs of *Lear* be alleviated, or the charms and wit of *Rofalind* be abated by time. There is indeed nothing perifhable about him, except that very learning which he is faid fo much to want. He had not, it is true, enough for the demands of the age in which he lived, but he had perhaps too much for the reach

F   of

of his genius, and the intereft of his fame.
Milton and he will carry the decayed remnants
and fripperies of antient mythology into more
diftant ages than they are by their own force intitled to extend; and the metamorphofes of
Ovid, upheld by them, lay in a new claim to
unmerited immortality.

Shakefpeare is a name fo interefting, that it is
excufable to ftop a moment, nay it would be indecent to pafs him without the tribute of fome
admiration. He differs effentially from all other
writers: Him we may profefs rather to feel
than to underftand; and it is fafer to fay, on
many occafions, that we are poffeffed by him,
than that we poffefs him. And no wonder ;—
He fcatters the feeds of things, the principles
of character and action, with fo cunning a hand
yet with fo carelefs an air, and, mafter of our
feelings, fubmits himfelf fo little to our judgment,
that every thing feems fuperior. We difcern not
his courfe, we fee no connection of caufe and effect,

lect, we are rapt in ignorant admiration, and
claim no kindred with his abilities. All the
incidents; all the parts, look like chance; whilst
we feel and are senfible that the whole is de-
sign. His Characters not only act and speak
in strict conformity to nature, but in strict
relation to us; just so much is shewn as is re-
quisite, just so much is impressed; he com-
mands every passage to our heads and to our
hearts, and moulds us as he pleases, and that
with so much ease, that he never betrays his
own exertions. We see these Characters act from
the mingled motives of passion, reason, in-
terest, habit and complection, in all their proportions, when they are supposed to know it
not themselves; and we are made to acknowledge that their actions and sentiments are, from
those motives, the necessary result. He at
once blends and distinguishes every thing;—
every thing is complicated, every thing is plain;
I restrain the further expressions of my admiration lest they should not seem applicable

to

to man; but it is really aftonifhing that a
mere human being, a part of humanity only,
fhould fo perfectly comprehend the whole;
and that he fhould poffefs fuch exquifite
art, that whilft every woman and every child
fhall feel the whole effect, his learned Editors
and Commentators fhould yet fo very frequently
miftake or feem ignorant of the caufe. A
fceptre or a ftraw are in his hands of equal effi-
cacy; he needs no felection; he converts every
thing into excellence; nothing is too great,
nothing is too bafe. Is a character efficient
like *Richard*, it is every thing we can wifh:
Is it otherwife, like *Hamlet*, it is productive
of equal admiration: Action produces one
mode of excellence and inaction another: The
Chronicle, the Novel, or the Ballad; the king,
or the beggar, the hero, the madman, the fot
or the fool; it is all one;—nothing is worfe, nothing is better: The fame genius pervades and
is equally admirable in all. Or, is a character
to be fhewn in progreffive change, and the events

of

of years comprized within the hour ;—with what a Magic hand does he prepare and fcatter his fpells! The Underftanding muft, in the firft place, be fubdued; and lo! how the rooted prejudices of the child fpring up to confound the man! The Weird fifters rife, and order is extinguifhed. The laws of nature give way, and leave nothing in our minds but wildnefs and horror. No paufe is allowed us for reflection : Horrid fentiment, furious guilt and compunction, air-drawn daggers, murders, ghofts, and inchantment, fhake and *poffefs us wholly.* In the mean time the *procefs* is completed. *Macbeth* changes under our eye, *the milk of human kindnefs is converted to gall; he has fupped full of horrors,* and his *May of life is fallen into the fear, the yellow leaf;* whilft we, the fools of amazement, are infenfible to the fhifting of place and the lapfe of time, and till the curtain drops, never once wake to the truth of things, or recognize the laws of exiftence.— On fuch an occafion, a fellow, like *Rymer,*

waking

waking from his trance, shall lift up his Con-
stable's staff, and charge this great Magician,
this daring *practicer of arts inhibited*, in the name
of *Ariftotle*, to furrender; whilst *Ariftotle* himfelf, difowning his wretched Officer, would
fall proftrate at his feet and acknowledge his
fupremacy.---O fupreme of Dramatic excellence! (*might he fay*,) not to me be imputed the
infolence of fools. The bards of *Greece* were
confined within the narrow circle of the Chorus,
and hence they found themfelves conftrained to
practice, for the moft part, the precifion, and
copy the details of nature. I followed them,
and knew not that a larger circle might be
drawn, and the Drama extended to the whole
reach of human genius. Convinced, I fee that
a more compendious *nature* may be obtained;
a nature of *effects* only, to which neither the
relations of place, or continuity of time, are always effential. Nature, condefcending to the
faculties and apprehenfions of man, has drawn
through

through human life a regular chain of vifible caufes and effects: But Poetry delights in furprize, conceals her fteps, feizes at once upon the heart, and obtains the Sublime of things without betraying the rounds of her afcent: True Poefy is *magic,* not *nature*; an effect from caufes hidden or unknown. To the Magician I prefcribed no laws; his law and his power are one; his power is his law. Him, who neither imitates, nor is within the reach of imitation, no precedent can or ought to bind, no limits to contain. If his end is obtained, who fhall queftion his courfe? Means, whether apparent or hidden, are juftified in Poefy by fuccefs; but then moft perfect and moft admirable when moft concealed *.---But

F 4 whither

---

* Thefe obfervations have brought me fo near to the regions of Poetic *magic,* (ufing the word here in its ftrict and proper fenfe, and not loofely as in the *text*) that tho' they lie not directly in my courfe, I yet may
be

whither am I going! This copious and do-
lightful topic has drawn me far beyond my
defign : I haften back to my fubject, and am
guarded, for a time at leaft, againft any further temptation to digrefs.

I was

be allowed in this place to point the reader that way.
A felt propriety, or truth of art, from an unfeen, tho'
fuppofed adequate caufe, we call *nature.* A like feeling of propriety and truth, fuppofed without a caufe,
or as feeming to be derived from caufes inadequate,
fantaftic, and abfurd,--fuch as wands, circles, incanta-
tions, and fo forth,---we call by the general name
magic, including all the train of fuperftition, witches,
ghofts, fairies, and the reft.--*Reafon* is confined to the
line of vifible exiftence ; our *paffions* and our *fancy*
extend far beyond into the *obfcure* ; but however lawlefs their operations may feem, the images they fo
wildly form have yet a relation to truth, and are the
fhadows at leaft, however fantaftic, of *reality.* I am
not inveftigating but paffing this fubject, and muft
therefore leave behind me much curious fpeculation.
Of Perfonifications however we fhould obferve that
thofe which are made out of abftract ideas are the
creatures of the Underftanding only : Thus, of the
mixed

I was confidering the dignity of *Falſtaff* ſo
far as it might ſeem connected with, or productive of military merit, and I have affigned
him *reputation* at leaſt, if not *fame*, noble
connection, birth, attendants, title, and an honourable

mixed modes, virtue, beauty, wiſdom and others,---
what are they but very obſcure ideas of *qualities* conſidered as abſtracted from any *ſubject* whatever ? The
mind cannot ſteadily contemplate ſuch an abſtrac-
tion : What then does it do?---Invent or imagine a ſubject in order to ſupport theſe qualities;
and hence we get the Nymphs or Goddeſſes of virtue, of beauty, or of wiſdom; the very ob-
ſcurity of the ideas being the cauſe of their con-
verſion into ſenſible objects, with preciſion both of
feature and of form. But as reaſon has its perſonifi-
cations, ſo has *paſſion.*---Every paſſion has its Object,
tho' often diſtant and obſcure;---to be brought nearer
then, and rendered more diſtinct, it is perſonified;
and Fancy fantaſtically decks, or aggravates the *form*,
and adds " a local habitation and a name. " But paſſion is the *dupe* of its own artifice and *realiſes* the
image it had formed. The Grecian theology was mixed of both theſe kinds of perſonification. Of the images
produced by paſſion it muſt be obſerved that they are
the

nourable penfion; every one of them prefump-
tive proofs of Military merit, and motives of
action. What deduction is to be made on
thefe articles, and why they are fo much obfcured may, perhaps, hereafter appear.

I have

the images, for the moft part, not of the paffions
themfelves, but of their remote effects. *Guilt* looks
through the medium, and beholds a devil; *fear*, fpec-
tres of every fort; *hope*, a fmiling cherub; *malice* and
envy fee hags, and witches, and inchanters dire;
whilft the innocent and the young, behold with fearful delight the tripping fairy, whofe fhadowy form the
moon gilds with its fofteft beams.——Extravagant as
all this appears, it has its laws fo precife that we
are fenfible both of a local and temporary, and of an
univerfal magic; the firft derived from the general nature of the human mind, influenced by particular habits,
inftitutions, and climate; and the latter from the fame
general nature abftracted from thofe confiderations;
Of the firft fort the *machinery* in *Macbeth* is a very
ftriking inftance; a machinery, which, however exquifite at the time, has already loft more than half its
force; and the Gallery now laughs in fome places
where it ought to fhudder:——But the magic of the
Tempeft is lafting and univerfal.

There

I have now gone through the examination of
all the perfons of the Drama from whofe mouths
any thing can be drawn relative to the Courage of *Falftaff*, excepting the *Prince* and *Poins*,
whofe evidence I have begged leave to *referve*,
and

There is befides a fpecies of writing for which we
have no term of art, and which holds a middle place
between nature and magic ; I mean where fancy either
alone, or mingled with reafon, or reafon affuming the
appearance of fancy, governs fome real exiftence ; but
the whole of this art is pourtrayed in a fingle Play ;
in the real madnefs of *Lear*, in the affumed wildnefs
of *Edgar*, and in the Profeffional *Fantafque* of the *Fool*,
all operating to contraft and heighten each other.
There is yet another feat in this kind, which *Shakefpeare* has performed ;--he has perfonified *malice* in his
Caliban ; a character kneaded up of three diftinct natures, the diabolical, the human, and the brute.
The reft of his preternatural beings are images of
effects only, and cannot fubfift but in a furrounding
atmofphere of thofe paffions, from which they are derived. *Caliban* is the paffion itfelf, or rather a compound of malice, fervility, and luft, *fubftantiated* ; and
therefore beft fhewn in contraft with the lightnefs of

Ariel

and excepting a very fevere cenfure paffed on
him by Lord *John* of *Lancafter*, which I fhall
prefently confider: But I muft firft obferve,
that fetting afide the jefts of the *Prince* and *Poins*,
and this cenfure of *Lancafter*, there is not one
expreffion

Ariel and the innocence of *Miranda.---Witches* are
fometimes fubftantial exiftences, fuppofed to be poffeffed
by, or allyed to the unfubftantial; but the Witches
in *Macbeth* are a grofs fort of fhadows, " bubbles of the
earth," as they are finely called by *Banquo.---Ghofts*
differ from other imaginary beings in this, that they
belong to no element, have no fpecific nature or character, and are effects, however harfh the expreffion,
fuppofed without a caufe; the reafon of which is that
they are not the creation of the poet, but the fervile
copies or tranfcripts of popular imagination, connected with fuppofed reality and religion. Should the
poet affign the true caufe, and call them the mere paint-
ing or *coinage of the brain*, he would difappoint his
own end, and deftroy the being he had raifed. Should
he affign fictitious caufes, and add a fpecific nature, and
a local habitation, it would not be endured; or the
effect would be loft by the converfion of one being
into another. The approach to reality in this cafe
defeats

expreffion uttered by any character in the Drama
that can be conftrued into any impeachment of
Falftaff's Courage;—an obfervation made before
as refpecting fome of the Witneffes; — it is
now extended to all : And though this filence
be a negative proof only, it cannot, in my opinion, under the circumftances of the cafe, and
whilft uncontradicted by facts, be too much re-
lied on. If *Falftaff* had been intended for the
character of a *Miles Gloriofus*, his behaviour
ought, and therefore would have been com-
mented upon by others. *Shakefpeare* feldom
trufts to the apprehenfions of his audience; his
characters interpret for one another continually,
and when we leaft fufpect fuch artful and fecret

management

defeatsall the arts and managements of fiction.---The
whole play of the *Tempeft* is of fo high and fuperior a
nature that *Dryden*, who had attempted to imitate in
vain, might well exclaim that

" - ---*Shakefpeare*'s *magic* could not copied be,
" Within that circle none durft walk but He. "

management: The conduct of *Shakespeare* in this respect is admirable, and I could point out a thousand passages which might put to shame the advocates of a formal Chorus, and prove that there is as little of neceffity as grace in so mechanic a contrivance *. But I confine my censure of the Chorus to its suppofed use of comment and interpretation only.

Falstaff is, indeed, so far from appearing to my eye in the light of a *Miles Gloriofus*, that in the beft of my tafte and judgment, he does not difcover, except in confequence of the robbery, the leaft *trait* of fuch a character. All his boafting fpeeches are humour, mere humour, and carefully fpoken to perfons who cannot mifapprehend them, who cannot be impofed on : They contain indeed, for the moft part, an unreafonable and imprudent ridicule of

* Ænobarbus, in Anthony and Cleopatra is in effect the Chorus of the Play; as Menenius Agrippa is of Coriolanus.

of himfelf, the ufual fubject of his good humoured merriment; but in the company of ignorant people, fuch as the Juftices, or his own
followers, he is remarkably referved, and does
not hazard any thing, even in the way of humour, that may be fubject to miftake : Indeed
he no where feems to fufpect that his character
is open to cenfure on this fide, or that he
needs the arts of impofition.---*" Turk Gregory*
" never did fuch deeds in arms as I have done this
" day," is fpoken, whilft he breathes from action,
to the Prince in a tone of jolly humour, and
contains nothing but a light ridicule of his
own inactivity : This is as far from real boafting as his faying before the battle, *" Wou'd it*
" were bedt-ime, Hal, *and all were well,"* is from
meanefs or depreffion: This articulated wifh
is not the the fearful outcry of a *Coward,* but the
frank and honeft breathing of a *generous fellow,*
who does not expect to be ferioufly reproached
with the character. Inftead indeed, of deferving the name of a vain glorious *Coward,* his

modefty

modefty perhaps on this head, and whimfical
ridicule of himfelf, have been a principal fource
of the imputation.

But to come to the very ferious reproach
thrown upon him by that *cold blooded* boy, as
he calls him, *Lancaster.*------*Lancaster* makes a
folemn treaty of peace with the *Archbifhop of
York, Mowbray,* &c. upon the faith of which
they difperfe their troops; which is no fooner
done than *Lancaster* arrefts the Principals; and
purfues the *fcattered ftray :* A tranfaction, by
the bye, fo fingularly perfidious, that I wifh
Shakefpeare, for his own credit, had not fuffered it to pafs under his pen without marking
it with the blackeft ftrokes of Infamy.---Dur-
ing this tranfaction, *Falftaff* arrives, joins in
the purfuit, and takes Sir *John Coleville* prifoner. Upon being feen by *Lancaster* he is thus
addreffed :------

" *Now*

" *Now Falſtaff, where have you been all this while?*
" *When every thing is over then you come :*
" *Theſe tardy tricks of yours will, on my life,*
" *One time or other break ſome gallows' back.*"

This may appear to many a very formidable paſſage. It is ſpoken, as we may ſay, in
the hearing of the army, and by one intitled]
as it were by his ſtation to decide on military
conduct; and if no puniſhment immediately
follows, the forbearance may be imputed to
a regard for the Prince of Wales, whoſe favour
the delinquent was known ſo unworthily to poſſeſs. But this reaſoning will by no means apply to the real circumſtances of the caſe. The
effect of this paſſage will depend on the credit we ſhall be inclined to give to *Lancaſter*
for integrity and candour, and ſtill more upon
the facts which are the ground of this cenſure,
and which are fairly offered by *Shakeſpeare* to
our notice.

G   We

We will examine the evidence arifing from both ; and to this end we muft in the firft place a little unfold the character of this young Commander in chief ;---from a review of which we may more clearly difcern the general impulfes and fecret motives of his conduct : And this is a proceeding which I think the peculiar character of *Shakefpeare's* Drama will very well juftify.

We are already well prepared what to think of this young man :--We have juft feen a very pretty manœuvre of his in a matterof the higheft moment, and have therefore the lefs reafon to be furprized if we find him practifing a more petty fraud with fuitable fkill and addrefs. He appears in truth to have been what *Falftaff* calls him, *a cold referved fober-blooded boy* ; a politician, as it fhould feem, by nature ; bred up moreover in the fchool of *Bolingbroke* his father, and tutored to betray : With fufficient courage and ability perhaps, but with too much of the knave

knave in his compofition, and too little of
enthufiafm, ever to be a great and fuperior character. That fuch a youth as this fhould,
even from the propenfities of character alone,
take any plaufible occafion to injure a frank
unguarded man of wit and pleafure, will not
appear unnatural. But he had other induce-
ments. *Falftaff* had given very general fcandal
by his diftinguifhed wit and noted poverty,
infomuch that a little cruelty and injuftice
towards him was likely to pafs, in the eye of
the grave and prudent part of mankind, as a
very creditable piece of fraud, and to be accounted to *Lancafter* for virtue and good fervice. But *Lancafter* had motives yet more prevailing; *Falftaff* was a Favourite, without the
power which belongs to that character; and
the tone of the Court was ftrongly againft him,
as the mifleader and corrupter of the Prince;
who was now at too great a diftance to afford
him immediate countenance and protection.
A fcratch then, between jeft and earneft as it

were,

were, fomething that would not too much offend the prince, yet would leave behind a difgraceful fcar upon *Falftaff*, was very fuitable
to the temper and fituation of parties and affairs. With thefe obfervations in our thought
let us return to the paffage : It is plainly intended for difgrace, but how artful, how cautious, how infidious is the manner! It may
pafs for fheer pleafantry and humour : *Lancafter*
affumes the familiar phrafe and *girding* tone
of *Harry*; and the gallows, as he words it,
appears to be in the moft danger from an encounter with *Falftaff*.---With refpect to the matter, 'tis a kind of *mitching malicho*; it means
mifchief indeed, but there is not precifion enough
in it to intitle it to the appellation of a formal
charge, or to give to *Falftaff* any certain and
determined ground of defence. *Tardy tricks* may
mean, not Cowardice but neglect only, though
the *manner* may feem to carry the imputation to both.---The reply of *Falftaff* is exactly
fuited to the qualities of the fpeech;-----for

Falftaff

Falstaff never wants ability but conduct only.
He anſwers the general effect of this ſpeech,
by a feeling and ſerious complaint of injuſ-
tice; he then goes on to apply his defence to
the vindication both of his diligence and courage; but he deſerts by degrees his ſerious tone,
and taking the handle of pleaſantry which
Lancaſter had held forth to him, he is pru-
dently content, as being ſenſible of *Lancaſter*'s
high rank and ſtation, to let the whole paſs off
in buffoonery and humour. But the queſtion
is, however, not concerning the adroitneſs and
management of either party : Our buſineſs is,
after putting the credit of *Lancaſter* out of the
queſtion, to diſcover what there may be of truth
and of fact either in the charge of the one, or
the defence of the other. From this only,
we ſhall be able to draw our inferences with
fairneſs and with candour. The charge againſt
Falſtaff is already in the poſſeſſion of the reader : The defence follows.---

G 3   Falſ.

Falſ. " *I would be ſorry, my lord, but it ſhould*
" *be thus : I never knew yet but that rebuke and*
" *check were the reward of valour. Do you think*
" *me a ſwallow, an arrow, or a bullet ? Have I*
" *in my poor and old motion the expedition of*
" *thought ? I ſpeeded hither within the very ex-*
" *tremeſt inch of poſſibility. I have foundered nine-*
" *ſcore and odd poſts,* (deſerting by degrees his
" ſerious tone, for *one* of more addreſs and ad-
" vantage) *and here travel-tainted as I am, have I*
" *in my pure and immaculate valour taken Sir John*
" *Coleville of the dale, a moſt furious Knight and*
" *valorous enemy.*"

Falſtaff's anſwer then is, that he uſed all poſſible expedition to join the army ; the not
doing of which, with an implication of Cowardice as the cauſe, is the utmoſt extent of
the charge againſt him ; and to take off this
implication he refers to the evidence of a fact
preſent and manifeſt,---the ſurrender of *Coleville* ;
in whoſe hearing he ſpeaks, and to whom
therefore

therefore he his fuppofed to appeal. Nothing then remains but that we fhould inquire if *Falftaff*'s anfwer was really founded in truth; " *I fpeeded hither*, fays he, *within the extremeft inch* " *of poffibility:* " If it be fo, he is juftified : But I am afraid, for we muft not conceal any thing, that *Faftaff* was really detained too long by his debaucheries in London; at leaft, if we take the Chief Juftice's words very ftrictly.

" Ch. Juft. *How now, Sir John ? What are you* " *brawling here? Doth this become your* PLACE, *your* " TIME, *your* BUSINESS ? *You fhould have been well* " *on your way to York.*"

Here then feems to be a delay worthy perhaps of rebuke; and if we could fuppofe *Lancafter* to mean nothing more by *tardy tricks* than idlenefs and debauch, I fhould not poffibly think myfelf much concerned to vindicate *Falftaff* from the charge; but the words imply, to my apprehenfion, a defigned and deliberate

G 4   avoidance

avoidance of danger. Yet to the contrary of
this we are furnifhed with very full and complete evidence. *Falftaff*, the moment he quits
London, difcovers the utmoft eagernefs and im-
patience to join the army; he gives up his
gluttony, his mirth, and his eafe. We fee him
take up in his paffage fome recruits at *Shallow's*
houfe; and tho' he has pecuniary views upon
Shallow, no inducement ftops him; he takes
no refrefhment, he cannot *tarry dinner*, he hurries off; " *I will not*, fays he to the Juftices,
" *ufe many words with you. Fare ye well Gentle-*
" *men both; I thank ye, I muft a dozen miles to*
night."---He mifufes, it is true, at this time the
King's Prefs damnably; but that does not concern me, at leaft not for the prefent; it belongs to
other parts of his character.---It appears then
manifeftly that *Shakefpeare* meant to fhew
Falftaff as really ufing the utmoft fpeed in his
power; he arrives almoft literally *within the*
extremeft inch of poffibility; and if *Lancafter* had
not accelerated the event by a ftroke of perfidy
　　　　　　　　　　　 · much

much more fubject to the imputation of
Cowardice than the *Debauch* of *Falftaff,* he
would have been time enough to have fhared
in the danger of a fair and honeft decifion.
But great men have it feems a priviledge;
" *that in the* General's *but a choleric word,*
" *which in the* Soldier *were flat blafphemy.*"
Yet after all, *Falftaff* did really come time
enough, as it appears, to join in the villain-
ous triumphs of the day, to take prifoner
*Coleville of the dale, a moft furious Knight and
valorous enemy.*---Let us look to the fact.
If this incident fhould be found to contain
any ftriking proof of *Falftaff's* Courage and
Military fame, his defence againft *Lancafter*
will be ftronger than the reader has even a
right to demand. *Falftaff* encounters *Coleville* in
the field, and having demanded his name,
is ready to affail him ; but *Coleville* afks him
if he is not Sir *John Falftaff;* thereby implying
a purpofe of furrender. *Falftaff* will not fo much
as furnifh him with a pretence, and anfwers
only,

only, that *he is as good a man.* " *Do you yield Sir,
or ſhall I ſweat for you ?* " *I think,* ſays Coleville
" *you are Sir John Falſtaff, and in that thought*
" *yield me.*" This fact, and the incidents
with which it is accompanied, ſpeak loudly ;
it ſeems to have been contrived by the author on purpoſe to take off a rebuke ſo autho-
ritatively made by *Lancaſter.* The fact is ſet
before our eyes to confute the cenſure : *Lancaſter* himſelf ſeems to give up his charge,
tho' not his ill will ; for upon *Falſtaff*'s aſking
leave to paſs through Gloſterſhire, and artfully deſiring that, upon *Lancaſter*'s return to
Court, *he might ſtand well in his report, Lancaſter* ſeems in his anſwer to mingle malice
and acquital. " *Fare ye well,* Falſtaff, *I in my*
" *condition ſhall better ſpeak of you than you*
" *deſerve. I would,* ſays Falſtaff, who is left
behind in the ſcene, . " *You had but the*
" *wit ; 'twere better than your Dukedom.*" He
continues on the ſtage ſome time chewing the
cud of diſhonour, which, with all his facility,

he

he cannot well fwallow. "*Good faith*" fays he, accounting to himfelf as well as he could for the injurious conduct of *Lancafter*; "*this* "*fober-blooded boy does not love me.*" This he might well believe. "*A man*, fays he, *cannot* "*make him laugh*; *there's none of thefe demure* "*boys come to any proof; but that's no marvel,* "*they drink no fack.*"---*Falftaff* then it feems knew no drinker of fack who was a Coward; at leaft the inftance was not home and famiiiar to him.---"*They all*, fays he, *fall into a kind* "*of Male green ficknefs, and are generally fools and* *Cowards.*" Anger has a privilege, and I think *Falftaff* has a right to turn the tables upon *Lancafter* if he can; but *Lancafter* was certainly no fool, and I think upon the whole, no Coward; yet the Male green ficknefs which *Falftaff* talks of, feems to have infected his manners and afpect, and taken from him all external indication of gallantry and courage. He behaves in the battle of Shrewfbury beyond the promife of his complexion and deportment:

"*By*

" *By heaven thou haſt deceived me Lancaſter,* ſays Harry, "*I did not think thee Lord of ſuch a ſpirit!* Nor was his father leſs ſurprized " *at his holding Lord Percy at the point with luſtier maintenance than he did look for from ſuch an unripe warrior.*" But how well and unexpectedly ſoever he might have behaved upon that occaſion, he does not ſeem to have been of a temper to truſt fortune too much or too often with his ſafety; therefore it is that, in order to keep the event in his own hands, he loads the Die, in the preſent caſe, with villainy and deceit: The event however he piouſly aſcribes, like a wiſe and prudent youth as he is, without paying that worſhip to himſelf which he ſo juſtly merits, to the ſpecial favour and interpoſition of Heaven.

" *Strike up your drums, purſue the ſcattered ſtray.*
" *Heaven, and not we, have ſafely fought to-day.*"

But the prophane *Falſtaff,* on the contrary, leſs informed and leſs ſtudious of ſupernatural things,

things, imputes the whole of this conduct to
thin potations, and the not drinking largely of
good and excellent *fherris*; and fo little doubt
does he feem to entertain of the Cowardice and
ill difpofition of this youth, that he ftands
devifing caufes, and cafting about for an hypo-
thefis on which the whole may be phyfically
explained and accounted for ;---but I fhall leave
him and Doctor *Cadogan* to fettle that point
as they may.

The only ferious charge againft *Falftaff's* Courage, we have now at large examined ; it came
from great authority, from the Commander in
chief, and was meant as chaftifement and rebuke ; but it appears to have been founded in ill-
will, in the particular character of *Lancafter*, and
in the wantonnefs and infolence of power; and the
author has placed near, and under our notice,
full and ample proofs of its injuftice.--And thus
the deeper we look unto *Falftaff's* character, the
ftronger is our conviction that he was not intended

tended to be shewn as a Conftitutional coward: Cenfure cannot lay fufficient hold on him,---and even malice turns away, and more than half pronounces his acquittal.

But as yet we have dealt principally in parole and circumftantial evidence, and have referred to *Fact* only incidentally. But *Facts* have a much more operative influence : They may be produced, not as arguments only, but Records ; not to difpute alone, but to decide.---It is time then to behold *Falftaff* in actual fervice as a foldier, in danger, and in battle. We have already difplayed one fact in his defence againft the cenfure of *Lancafter* ; a fact extremely unequivocal and decifive. But the reader knows I have others, and doubtlefs goes before me to the action at *Shrewfbury.* In the midft and in the heat of battle we fee him come forwards ;---what are his words ? " *I* " *have led my Rag-o-muffians where they are peppered;* " *there's not three of my hundred and fifty left alive.*"

But

But to *whom* does he fay this? To himfelf
only; he fpeaks *in foliloquy.* There is no
queftioning the fact, *he had* led *them; they
were peppered; there were not* three *left alive.* He
was in luck, being in bulk equal to any two
of them, to efcape unhurt. Let the author
anfwer for that, I have nothing to do with it:
He was the Poetic maker of the whole *Corps,*
and he might difpofe of them as he pleafed.
Well might the Chief juftice, as we now find,
acknowledge *Falftaff's* fervices in this day's battle; an acknowledgment, which amply confirms
the fact. A Modern officer, who had performed a feat of this kind, would expect,
not only the praife of having done his duty,
but the appellation of a hero. But poor *Falftaff* has too much wit to thrive: In fpite of
probability, in fpite of inference, in fpite of
fact, he muft be a Coward ftill. He happens
unfortunately to have more Wit than Courage, and therefore we are malicioufly determined that he fhall have no Courage at all.
But let us fuppofe that his modes of expref-

fion

fion, even *in foliloquy*, will admit of fome
abatement;—how much fhall we abate? Say
that he brought off *fifty* inftead of *three*; yet
a Modern captain would be apt to look big
after an action with two thirds of his men,
as it were, in his belly. Surely *Shakefpeare* never
meant to exhibit this man as a Conftitutional
coward; if he did, his means were fadly de-
ftructive of his end. We fee him, after he
had expended his Rag-o-muffians, with fword
and target in the midft of battle, in perfect
poffeffion of himfelf, and replete with humour
and jocularity. He was, I prefume, in fome
immediate perfonal danger, in danger alfo of
a general defeat; too corpulent for flight;
and to be led a prifoner was probably to be
led to execution; yet we fee him laughing
and eafy, offering a bottle of fack to the
Prince inftead of a piftol, punning, and telling him, " *there was that which would* fack *a*
" *city.*"—" *What is it a time*, (fays the Prince)
" *to jeft and dally now ?*" No, a fober character
                                                     would

would not jeft on fuch an occafion, but a
Coward could not; he would neither have the
inclination, or the power. And what could fupport *Falftaff* in fuch a fituation? Not principle;
he is not fufpected of the Point of honour;
he feems indeed fairly to renounce it. " *Ho-*
" *nour cannot fet a leg or an arm ; it has no fkill in*
" *furgery :—What is it? a word only; meer air. It*
" *is infenfible to the dead; and detraction will not*
" *let it live with the living.*" What then, but
a ftrong natural conftitutional Courage, which
nothing could extinguifh or difmay?---In the following paffages the true character of *Falftaff* as to
Courage and Principle is finely touched, and
the different colours at once nicely blended
and diftinguifhed. " *If Percy be alive, I'll* pierce
" *him. If he do come in my way, fo :---If he*
" *do not, if I come in his willingly, let him make a*
" *Carbonado of me. I like not fuch grinning honour*
" *as Sir Walter hath; give me life; which, if I can*
" *fave, fo; if not, honour comes unlook'd for, and*
" *there's an eud.*" One cannot fay which pre-

H   vails

vails moſt here, profligacy or courage; they are both tinged alike by the ſame humour, and mingled in one common maſs; yet when we conſider the ſuperior force of *Percy*, as we muſt preſently alſo that of *Douglas*, we ſhall be apt, I believe, in our ſecret heart, to forgive him. Theſe paſſages are ſpoken in ſoliloquy and in battle : If every ſoliloquy made under ſimilar circumſtances were as audible as *Falſtaff*'s, the imputation might perhaps be found too general for cenſure. Theſe are among the paſſages that have impreſſed on the world an idea of Cowardice in *Falſtaff*;---yet why? He is reſolute to take his fate : If *Percy* do come in his way, *ſo*;--- if not, he will not ſeek inevitable deſtruction; he is willing to ſave his life, but if that cannot be, why,---" honour comes unlook'd for, and there's an end." This ſurely is not the language of Cowardice : It contains neither the Bounce or Whine of the character; he derides, it is true, and ſeems to renounce that grinning idol of Military zealots, *Honour*. But

Falſtaff

Falftaff was a kind of Military free-thinker; and has accordingly incurred the obloquy of his condition. He ftands upon the ground of natural Courage only and common fenfe, and has, it feems, too much wit for a hero.---But let me be well underftood;---I do not juftify *Falftaff* for renouncing the point of honour; it proceeded doubtlefs from a general relaxation of mind, and profligacy of temper. Honour is calculated to aid and ftrengthen natural courage, and lift it up to heroifm ; but natural courage, which can act as fuch without honour, is natural courage ftill; the very quality I wifh to maintain to *Falftaff.* And if, without the aid of honour, he can act with firmnefs, his portion is only the more eminent and dif- tinguifhed. In fuch a -character, it is to his actions, not his fentiments, that we are to look for conviction. But it may be ftill further urged in behalf of *Falftaff*, that there may be falfe honour as well as falfe religion. It is true ; yet even in that cafe, candour obliges

H 2

me

me to confefs, that the beft men are moft difpofed to conform, and moft likely to become the dupes of their own virtue. But it may however be more reafonably urged, that there are particular tenets both in honour and religion, which it is the grofsnefs of folly not to queftion. To feek out, to court affured deftruction, without leaving a fingle benefit behind, may be well reckoned in the number : And this is precifely the very folly which *Falftaff* feems to abjure ;---nor are we, perhaps intitled to fay more, in the way of cenfure, than that he had not virtue enough to become the dupe of honour, nor prudence enough to hold his tongue. I am willing however, if the reader pleafes, to compound this matter, and acknowledge, on my part, that *Falftaff* was in all refpects the *old foldier*; that he had put himfelf under the fober difcipline of difcretion, and renounced, in a great degree at leaft, what he might call, the Vanities and Superftitions of honour ; if the reader

will ·

will, on his part, admit that this might well be, without his renouncing, at the fame time, the natural firmnefs and refolution he was born to.

But there is a formidable objection behind. *Falftaff* counterfeits bafely on being attacked by *Douglas*; he affumes, in a cowardly fpirit, the appearance of death to avoid the reality. But there was no equality of force; not the leaft chance for victory, or life. And is it the duty then, *think we ftill*, of true Courage, to meet, without benefit to fociety, *certain death ?* Or is it only the phantafy of honour ?---But fuch a fiction is highly difgraceful;---true, and a man of nice honour might perhaps have *grinned* for it. But we muft remember that *Falftaff* had a double character; he was a *wit* as well as a *foldier*; and his Courage, however eminent, was but the *acceffary*; his wit was the *principal*; and the part, which, if they fhould come in competition, he had the

greateft

greateſt intereſt in maintaining. Vain indeed were
the licentiouſneſs of his principles, if he ſhould
ſeek death like a bigot, yet without the meed
of honour; when he might live by wit, and
encreaſe the reputation of that wit by living.
But why do I labour this point? It has been
already anticipated, and our improved acquaintance with *Falſtaff* will now require no
more than a ſhort narrative of the fact,

Whilſt in the battle of Shrewſbury he is
exhorting and encouraging the Prince who is
engaged with the *Spirit Percy*---"*Well ſaid Hal,
to him Hal,*"---he is himſelf attacked by the *Fiend
Douglas.* There was no match; nothing remained but death or ſtratagem; grinning honour, or laughing life. But an expedient
offers, a mirthful one,---Take your choice
Falſtaff, a point of honour, or a point of
drollery.---It could not be a queſtion;---
Falſtaff falls, *Douglas* is cheated, and the world
laughs. But does he fall like a Coward?

Nq

No, like a buffoon only; the superior principle prevails, and *Falstaff* lives by a stratagem growing out of his character, to prove
himself *no counterfeit*, to jest, to be employed,
and to fight again. That *Falstaff* valued himself, and expected to be valued by others,
upon this piece of saving wit is plain. It
was a stratagem, it is true; it argued pre-
sence of mind; but it was moreover, what
he most liked, a very laughable joke; and as
such he considers it; for he continues to counterfeit after the danger is over, that he may
also deceive the Prince, and improve the
event into more laughter. He might, for ought
that appears, have concealed the transaction;
the Prince was too earnestly engaged for ob-
servation; he might have formed a thousand
excuses for his fall; but he lies still and lis-
tens to the pronouncing of his epitaph by the
Prince with all the waggish glee and levity
of his character. The circumstance of his
wounding *Percy* in the thigh, and carrying
the

the dead body on his back like luggage, is *indecent* but not cowardly. The declaring, though in jeft, that he killed *Percy*, feems to me *idle*, but it is not meant or calculated for *impofition*; it is fpoken to the *Prince himfelf*, the man in the world who could not be, or be fuppofed to be impofed on. But we muft hear, whether to the purpofe or not, what it is that *Harry* has to fay over the remains of his old friend.

> *P. Hen.* What old acquaintance! could not
>   all this flefh
> Keep in a little life? Poor *Jack* farewell!
> I could have better fpared a better man.
> Oh! I fhou'd have a heavy mifs of thee,
> If I were much in love with vanity.
> Death hath not ftruck fo fat a *deer* to-day,
> Tho' many a *dearer* in this bloody fray;
> Imbowelled will I fee thee by and by;
> Till then, in blood by noble *Percy* lye.

This

This is wonderfully proper for the occafion;
it is affectionate, it is pathetic, yet it remembers
his vanities, and, with a faint gleam of recol-
lected mirth, even his plumpnefs and corpulency; but it is a pleafantry foftned and rendered even vapid by tendernefs, and it goes off
the fickly effort of a miferable pun*.---But to our
immediate purpofe,—why is not his Cowardice
remembered too? what no furprize that *Falftaff*

          fhould

* The cenfure commonly paffed on *Shakefpeare's puns,*
is, I think, not well founded. I remember but very
few, which are undoubtedly his, that may not be juf-
tifyed; and if *fo,* a greater inftance cannot be given
of the art which he fo peculiarly poffeffed of convert-
verting bafe things into excellence.

  " For if the Jew do cut but deep enough,
  " I'll pay the forfeiture *with all my heart.*"

A play upon words is the moft that can be expected
from one who affects gaiety under the preffure of fevere misfortunes; but fo imperfect, fo broken a gleam,

          can

fhould lye by the fide of the noble *Percy* in the bed of honour ! No reflection that flight, though unfettered by difeafe, could not avail; that fear could not find a fubterfuge from death ? Shall his corpulency and his vanities be recorded, and his more charaƈteriftic quality of Cowardice, even in the moment that it particularly demanded notice and reflection, be forgotten ? If by fparing a better man be here meant a *better foldier*, there is no doubt but there were better Soldiers in the army, more aƈtive, more young, more principled, more knowing; but none, it feems, taken for all in all, more acceptable. The comparative *better* ufed here leaves to *Falftaff* the praife at leaft of *good*; and to be a good foldier, is

can only ferve more plainly to difclofe the gloom and darknefs of the mind; it is an effort of fortitude, which failing in its operation, becomes the trueft, becaufe the moft unaffeƈted *pathos*; and a fkilful aƈtor, well managing his tone and aƈtion, might with this miferable pun, fteep a whole audience fuddenly in tears,

is to be a great way from Coward. But *Falſtaff's*
goodneſs, in this ſort, appears to have been not
only enough to redeem him from diſgrace, but
to mark him with reputation; if I was to add
with *eminence* and *diſtinction*, the funeral honours,
which are intended his obſequies, and his being
bid, till then, *to lye in blood by the noble Percy*,
would fairly bear me out.

Upon the whole of the paſſages yet before us,
why may I not reaſonably hope that the good
natured reader, (and I write to no other) not
offended at the levity of this exerciſe, may join
with me in thinking that the character of *Falſtaff*
as to valour, may be fairly and honeſtly ſummed
up in the very words which he himſelf uſes to
Harry; and which ſeem, as to this point, to be
intended by *Shakeſpeare* as a *Compendium* of his
character. "*What*, ſays the Prince, *a Coward
Sir John Paunch!*" *Falſtaff* replies, "*Indeed I
am not* John of Gaunt *your grandfather, but yet*
"*no Coward, Hal.*"

The

The robbery at *Gadſhill* comes now to be conſidered. But *here,* after ſuch long argumenta-
tion, we may be allowed to breath a little.

I know not what Impreſſion has been made
on the reader ; a good deal of evidence has been
produced, and much more remains to be offered.
But how many ſorts of men are there whom
no evidence can perſuade! How many, who
ignorant of *Shakeſpeare,* or forgetful of the text,
may as well read heathen Greek, or the laws
of the land, as this unfortunate Commentary?
How many, who proud and pedantic, hate all
novelty, and damn it without mercy under one
compendious word, Paradox? How many more,
who not deriving their opinions immediately
from the ſovereignty of reaſon, hold at the will
of ſome ſuperior lord, to whom accident or inclination has attached them, and who, true to
their vaſſalage, are reſolute not to ſurrender,
without expreſs permiſſion, their baſe and ill-
gotten poſſeſſions. Theſe, however habited, are
the

the mob of mankind, who hoot and holla, hifs
or huzza, juft as their various leaders may direct. I *challenge* the whole Pannel as not holding by free tenure, and therefore not competent
to the purpofe either of condemnation or acquittal. But to the men of very nice honour what
fhall be faid ? I fpeak not of your men of good
fervice, but fuch as Mr. * * * * " *Souls made
of fire*, and *children of the fun*." Thefe gentlemen,
I am fadly afraid, cannot in honour or prudence
admit of any compofition in the very nice article of Courage ; *fufpicion* is *difgrace*, and they
cannot ftay to parley with difhonour. The mif-
fortune in cafes of this kind, is, that it is not
eafy to obtain a fair and impartial Jury : When
we cenfure others with an eye to our own ap-
plaufe, we are as feldom´fparing of reproach,
as inquifitive into circumftance; and bold is
the man, who tenacious of juftice, fhall venture
to weigh circumftances, or draw lines of diftinction between Cowardice and any apparently fimi-
lar or neighbour quality : As Well may a lady,

virgin

virgin or matron, of immaculate honour, prefume to pity or palliate the foft failing of fome
unguatded friend, and thereby confefs, as it were,
thofe fympathetic feelings which it behoves her
to conceal under the moft contemptuous difdain ;
a difdain, always proportioned, I believe, to a
certain confciou[nefs which we muft not explain.
I am afraid that poor *Falftaff* has fuffered not a
little, and may yet fuffer by this faftidioufnefs of
temper. But though we may find thefe claffes
of men rather unfavourable to our wiflics, the
Ladies, one may hope, whofe fmiles are moft
worth our ambition, may be found more pro-
pitious ; yet they too, through a generous conformity to the *brave*, are apt to take up the high
tone of honour. Heroifm is an idea perfectly
conformable to the natural delicacy and ele-
vation of their minds. Should we be fortunate
enough therefore to redeem *Falftaff* from the imputations of Cowardice, yet plain Courage, I
am afraid, will not ferve the turn : Even their
heroes, I think, muft be for the moft part in the

bloom

bloom of youth, or *juft where youth ends, in man-hood's frefheft prime*; but to be " *Old, cold, and of* " *intolerable entrails; to be fat and greafy; as poor* " *as Job, and as flanderous as Satan* ;"—Take him away, he merits not a fair trial; he is too of-fenfive to be turned, too odious to be touched. I grant, indeed that the fubject of our lecture is not without his infirmity ; " *He cuts three in-* " *ches on the ribs, he was fhort-winded,*" and his breath poffibly not of the fweeteft : " *He had the* " *gout,*" or fomething worfe, " *which played the* " *rogue with his great toe.*"—But thefe confidera-tions are not to the point ; we fhall conceal, as much as may be, thefe offences ; our bufinefs is with his *heart* only, which, as we fhall endeavour to demonftrate, lies in the right place, and is firm and found, notwithftanding a few indica-tions to the contrary.—As for you, *Mrs.* MON-TAGUE, I am grieved to find that *you* have been involved in a Popular error ; fo much you muft allow me to fay ;—for the reft, I bow to your genius and your virtues : You have given to the world

world a very elegant compófition; and I am told your manners and your mind are yet more pure, more elegant than your book. *Falſtaff* was too grofs, too infirm, for your infpection; but if you durſt have looked nearer, you would not have found Cowardice in the number of his infirmities.—We will try if we cannot redeem him from this univerfal cenfure.—Let the venal corporation of authors duck *to the golden fool*, let them ſhape their fordid quills to the mercenary ends of unmerited praife, or of bafer detraction;—*old Jack* though deferted by princes, though cenfured by an ungrateful world, and perfecuted from age to age by Critic and Commentator, and though never rich enough to hire one literary proſtitute, ſhall find a Voluntary defender; and that too at a time when the whole body of the *Nabobry* demands and requires defence; whilſt their ill-gotten and almoſt untold gold feels loofe in their unaſſured grafp, and whilſt they are ready to ſhake off portions of the enormous heap, that they may the more

fecurely

fecurely clafp the remainder.—But not to digrefs without end,—to the candid, to the
chearful, to the elegant reader we appeal;
our exercife is much too light for the four eye
of ftrict feverity ; it profeffes amufement only,
but we hope of a kind more rational than the
Hiftory of Mifs *Betfy*, eked out with the
Story of Mifs *Lucy*, and the Tale of Mr.
Twankum : And fo, in a leifure hour, and with
the good natured reader, it may be hoped,
to friend, we return, with an air as bufy and
important as if we were engaged in the grave
office of meafuring the *Pyramids*, or fettling
the antiquity of *Stonehenge*, to converfe with
this jovial, this fat, this roguifh, this frail,
but, I think, *not cowardly* companion.

Though the robbery at *Gads-Hill*, and the
fuppofed Cowardice of *Falftaff* on that occafion, are next to be confidered, yet I muft
previoufly declare, that I think the difcuffion
of this matter to be *now* uneffential to the

re-eftablifhment

re-eftablifhment of *Falftaff*'s reputation as a man of Courage. For fuppofe we fhould grant, in form, that *Faftaff* was furprized with fear in this fingle inftance, that he was off his guard, and even acted like a Coward ; what will follow, but that *Falftaff*, like greater heroes, had his weak moment, and was not exempted from panic and furprize ? If a fingle exception can deftroy a general character, *Hector* was a *Coward*, and *Anthony* a *Poltroon*. But for thefe feeming contradictions of Character we fhall feldom be at a lofs to account, if we carefully refer to circumftance and fituation.—In the prefent inftance, *Falftaff* had done an illegal act ; the exertion was over ; and he had unbent his mind in fecurity. The fpirit of enterprize, and the animating principle of hope, were withdrawn :—In this fituation, he is unexpectedly attacked ; he has no time to recall his thoughts, or bend his mind to action. He is not now acting in the Profeffion and in the Habits of a Soldier ;

Soldier; he is affociated with known Cowards; his affailants are vigorous, fudden, and bold; he is confcious of guilt; he has dangers to dread of every form, prefent and future; prifons and gibbets, as well as fword and fire; he is furrounded with darknefs, and the Sheriff, the Hangman, and the whole *Poffe Commitatus* may be at his heels :—Without a moment for reflection, is it wonderful that, under thefe circumftances, " *he should run and roar, and* " *carry his guts away with as much dexterity as* " *poffible ?*"

But though I might well reft the queftion on this ground, yet as there remains many good topics of vindication; and as I think a more minute inquiry into this matter will only bring out more evidence in fupport of *Falftaff*'s conftitutional Courage, I will not decline the difcuffion. I beg permiffion therefore to ftate fully, as well as fairly, the

whole

whole of this obnoxious tranfaction, this unfortunate robbery at *Gads-Hill.*

In the fcene wherein we become firft acquainted with *Falftaff*, his character is opened
in a manner worthy of *Shakefpeare :* We fee him
in a green old age, mellow, frank, gay, eafy,
corpulent, loofe, unprincipled, and luxurious;
a *Robber*, as he fays, *by his vocation;* yet not
altogether fo:—There was much, it feems, of
mirth and *recreation* in the cafe : " *The poor
abufes of the times,*" he wantonly and humouroufly
tells the Prince " *want countenance; and he hates
to fee refolution fobbed off, as it is, by the rufty
curb of old father antic, the law.* "—When he
quits the fcene, we are acquainted that he is
only paffing to the Tavern : " *Farewell,*" fays
he, with an air of carelefs jollity and gay content, " *You will find me in Eaft-Cheap.*" " *Fare-
" well,*" fays the Prince, " *thou latter fpring;
" farewell, all hallown fummer.*" But though all
this is excellent for *Shakefpeare's* purpofes, we
find

find, as yet at leaft, no hint of *Falftaff's* Cowardice, no appearance of Braggadocio, or any preparation whatever for laughter under this head.—The inftant *Falftaff* is withdrawn, *Poins* opens to the *Prince* his meditated fcheme of a double robbery; and here then we may reafonably expect to be let into thefe parts of *Falftaff's* character.—We fhall fee.

Poins. *Now my good fweet lord, ride with us to-*
" *morrow; I have a jeft to execute that I cannot*
" *manage alone.* Falftaff, Bardolph, Peto, *and*
" Gadfhill *fhall rob thofe men that we have already*
" *waylaid; yourfelf and I will not be there; and*
" *when they have the booty, if you and I do not*
" *rob them, cut this head from off my fhoulders."*

This is giving ftrong furety for his words; perhaps he thought the cafe required it: *But*
" *how,* fays the Prince, *fhall we part with them in*
" *fetting forth ?" Poins* is ready with his anfwer; he had matured the thought, and could folve

I 3 every

every difficulty :—" *They could set out before, or* " *after; their horses might be tied in the wood;* " *they could change their visors; and he had al-* " *ready procured cases of* buckram *to inmask their* " *outward garments."* This was going far; it was doing bufinefs in good earneft, But if we look into the Play we fhall be better able to account for this activity; we fhall find that there was, at leaft as much malice as jeft in *Poins's* intention, The rival fituations of *Poins* and *Falſtaff* had produced on both fides much jealoufy and ill will, which occafionally appears, in *Shakeſpeare's* manner, by fide lights, without confounding the main action; and by the little we fee of this *Poins,* he appears to be an unamiable, if not a very brutifh and bad, character.—But to pafs this ;---the Prince next fays, with a deliberate and wholefome caution, " *I doubt they will be too hard for us."* *Poins's* reply is remarkable; " *Well, for* two *of them, I know* " *them to be as true bred Cowards as ever turned back;* " *and for the* third, *if he fights longer than he*
" *fees*

" *fees caufe, I will forfwear arms.*" There is in this reply a great deal of management: There were *four* perfons in all, as *Poins* well knew, and he had himfelf, but a little before, named them,---*Falftaff, Bardolph, Peto,* and *Gadf-hill;* but now he omits one of the number, which muft be either *Falftaff,* as not fubject to any imputation in point of Courage; and in that cafe *Peto* will be the *third;*---or, as I rather think, in order to diminifh the force of the Prince's objection, he artfully drops *Gadfhill,* who was then out of town, and might there-fore be fuppofed to be lefs in the Prince's notice; and upon this fuppofition *Falftaff* will be the *third, who will not fight longer than he fees reafon.* But on either fuppofition, what evidence is there of a pre-fuppofed Cowar-dice in *Falftaff?* On the contrary, what ftronger evidence can we require that the Courage of *Falftaff* had to this hour, through various trials, ftood wholly unim-peached, than that *Poins,* the ill-difpofed *Poins,*

who

who ventures, for his own purpofes, to fteal, as it were, *one* of the *four* from the notice and memory of the Prince, and who fhews himfelf, from worfe motives, as fkilfull in *diminifhing* as *Falftaff* appears afterwards to be in *increafing* of numbers, than that this very *Poins* fhould not venture to put down *Falftaff* in the lift of Cowards; though the occafion fo ftrongly required that he fhould be degraded. What *Poins* dares do however in this fort, he *does.* " *As to the third,* " for fo he defcribes *Falftaff,* (as if the name of this Veteran would have excited too ftrongly the ideas of Courage and refiftance) " *if he fights longer than he fees reafon* " *I will forfwear arms."* This is the old trick of cautious and artful malice : The turn of exprcffion, or the tone of voice does all ; for as to the words thcmfelves, fimply con- dered, they might be now truly fpoken of almoft any man who ever lived, except the iron-headed hero of *Sweden.*---But *Poins* however adds fomething, which may appear more

decifive

decifive; " *The virtue of this jeſt will be, the*
" *incomprehenſible lyes which this fat rogue will*
" *tell when we meet at ſupper* ; *how thirty at*
" *leaſt he fought with* ; *and what wards, what*
" *blows, what extremities, he endured* : *And in the*
" *reproof of this lies the jeſt* :"---Yes, and the *ma-*
" *lice* too.—This prediction was unfortunately
fulfilled, even beyond the letter of it; a completion more incident, perhaps, to the predic-
tions of malice than of affection. But we
ſhall preſently ſee how far either the prediction, or the event, will go to the impeachment of *Falſtaff*'s Courage.---The Prince, who is
never duped, comprehends the whole of *Poins*'s
views. But let that paſs,

In the next ſcene we behold all the parties
at *Gads-Hill* in preparation for the robbèry.
Let us carefully examine if it contains any inti-
mation of Cowardice in *Falſtaff*. He is ſhewn
under a very ridiculous vexation about his
horſe, which is hid from him; but this is nothing

thing to the purpofe, or only proves that *Falftaff* knew no terror equal to that of walking
eight yards of uneven ground. But on occafion of
Gadfhill's being afked concerning the number
of the travellers, and having reported that they
were eight or ten,` Falftaff* exclaims, " *Zounds !*
" *will they not rob us !*" If he had faid more
.ferioufly, " *I doubt they will be too hard for us,*"---
he would then have only ufed the Prince's
own words upon a lefs alarming occafion.
This cannot need defence. But the Prince,
in his ufual ftile of mirth, replies, " *What a*
" *Coward, Sir John Paunch !*" To this one would
naturally expect from *Falftaff* fome light anfwer; but we are furprized with a very ferious one ;---" *I am not indeed* John of Gaunt *your*
" *grandfather, but yet no* Coward, Hal." This
is fingular : It contains, I think, the true character of *Falftaff*; and it feems to be thrown
out *here*, at a very critical conjuncture, as a
caution to the audience not to take too fadly
what was intended only (to ufe the Prince's
words)

words,) *" as argument for a week, laughter for* *" a month, and a good jeft for ever after."* The whole of *Falftaff's* paft life could not, it fhould feem, furnifh the Prince with a reply, and he is, therefore, obliged to draw upon the coming hope. *" Well,* (fays he, *myfterioufly,*) *" let the event try;"* meaning the event of the concerted attack on *Falftaff*; an event fo probable, that he might indeed venture to rely on it.—But the travellers approach: The Prince haftily propofes a divifion of ftrength; that he with *Poins* fhould take a ftation feperate from the reft, fo that if the travellers fhould efcape one party, they might light on the other: *Falftaff* does not objeft, though he fuppofes the travellefs to be eight or ten in number. We next fee *Falftaff* attack thefe travellers with alacrity ufing the accuftomed words of threat and terror;—they make no refiftance, and he binds and robs them.

Hitherto

Hitherto I think there has not appeared the leaſt *trait* either of boaſt or fear in *Falſtaff*. But now comes on the concerted tranſaction, which has been the ſource of ſo much diſhonour. *As they are ſharing the booty,* (ſays the ſtage direction) *the Prince and* Poins *ſet upon them, they all run away;* and Falſtaff *after a blow or two runs away too, leaving the booty behind them.*---" *Got with much eaſe :*" ſays the Prince, as an event beyond expectation, " *Now mer-* " *rily to horſe.*"---Poins adds, as they are going off, " *How the rogue roared !*" This obſervation is afterwards remembered by the Prince, who urging the jeſt to *Falſtaff,* ſays, doubtleſs with all the licence of exaggeration,--"*And you* Falſtaff, " *carried your guts away as nimbly, with as quick* " *dexterity, and roared for mercy, and ſtill ran* " *and roared, as I ever heard bull-calf.*" If he did roar for mercy, it muſt have been a very inarticulate ſort of roaring ; for there is not a ſingle word ſet down for *Falſtaff* from which this roaring may be inferred, or any ſtage direction

rection to the actor for that purpofe : But, in the fpirit of mirth and derifion, the lighteft exclamation might be eafily converted into the roar of a bull-calf.

We have now gone through this tranfaction confidered fimply on its own circumftances, and without reference to any future boaft · or imputation. It is upon thefe circumftances the cafe muft be tried, and every colour fub-fequently thrown on it, either by wit or folly, ought to be difcharged. Take it, then, as it ftands hitherto, with reference only to its own preceding and concomitant circumftances, and to the unbounded ability of *Shakefpeare* to obtain his own ends, and we muft, I think, be com-pelled to confefs that this tranfaction was ne-ver intended by *Shakefpear* to detect and ex-pofe the falfe pretences of a real Coward; but, on the contrary, to involve a man of allowed Courage, though in other refpects of a very peculiar character, in fuch circumftances and

fufpicions of Cowardice as might, by the operation of thofe peculiarities, produce afterwards
much temporary mirth among his familiar
and intimate companions : Of this we cannot
require a ftronger proof than the great attention which is paid to the decorum and truth
of character in the ftage direction already
quoted : It appears, from thence, that it was
not thought *decent* that *Falftaff* fhould run at all,
until he had been deferted by his companions,
and had even afterwards exchanged blows
with his affailants ;---and thus, a juft diftinction
is kept up between the natural Cowardice of
the three affociates and the accidental Terror
of *Falftaff*.

Hitherto, then, I think it is very clear
that no laughter either is, or is intended to
be, raifed upon the fcore of *Falftaff*'s Cowardice. For after all, it is not fingularly
ridiculous that an old inactive man of no
boaft, as far as appears, or extraordinary pre-
tenfions

tenſions to valour, ſhould endeavour to ſave himſelf by flight from the aſſault of two bold and vigorous aſſailants. The very Players, who are, I think, the very worſt judges of *Shakeſpeare*, have been made ſenſible, I ſuppoſe from long experience, that there is nothing in this tranſaction to excite any extraordinary laughter; but this they take to be a defect in the management of their author, and therefore I imagine it is, that they hold themſelves obliged to ſupply the vacancy, and fill it up with ſome low buffoonery of their own. Inſtead of the diſpatch neceſſary on this occaſion, they bring *Falſtaff, ſtuffing and all*, to the very front of the ſtage; where with much mummery and grimace, he ſeats himſelf down, with a canvaſs money-bag in his hand, to divide the ſpoil. In this ſituation he is attacked by the *Prince* and *Poins*, whoſe tin ſwords hang idly in the air and delay to ſtrike till the *Player Falſtaff*, who ſeems more troubled with flatulence than fear, is able to riſe; which

which is not till after some ineffectual efforts,
and with the affiftance, (to the beft of my
memory) of one of the thieves, who lingers
behind, in fpite of terror, for this friendly
purpofe; after which, without any refiftance on
his part, he is goaded off the ftage like a fat ox
for flaughter by thefe *ftony-hearted* drivers in
buckram. I think he does not *roar*;---perhaps
the player had never perfected himfelf in the
the tones of a bull-calf. This whole tranfaction fhould be fhewn between the interftices
of a back fcene: The lefs we fee in fuch
cafes, the better we conceive. Something of
refiftance and afterwards of celerity in flight
we fhould be made witneffes of; the *roar* we
fhould take on the credit of *Poins.* Nor is
there any occafion for all that bolftering with
which they fill up the figure of *Falftaff*; they
do not diftinguifh betwixt humourous exaggeration and neceffary truth. The Prince is
called *ftarveling*, *dried neat's tongue*, *ftock fifh*, and
other names of the fame nature. They might
with

with almoſt as good reaſon, ſearch the glaſs-
houſes for ſome exhauſted ſtoker to furniſh out
a Prince of *Wales* of ſufficient correſpondence
to this picture.

We next come to the ſcene of *Falſtaff's* braggadocioes. I have already wandered too much into
details ; yet I muſt, however, bring *Falſtaff* forward to this laſt ſcene of trial in all his proper
colouring and proportions. The progreſſive
diſcovery of *Falſtaff's* character is excellently
managed.—In the firſt ſcene we become acquainted with his figure, which we muſt in ſome
degree conſider as a part of his character ; we
hear of his gluttony and his debaucheries, and
become witneſſes of that indiſtinguiſhable mix-
ture of humour and licentiouſneſs which runs
through his whole character ; but what we are
principally ſtruck with, is the eaſe of his
manners and deportment, and the unaffected
freedom and wonderful pregnancy of his wit
and humour. We ſee him, in the next ſcene, agi-

K   tated

tated with vexation : His horfe is concealed
from him, and he gives on this occafion fo
ftriking a defcription of his diftrefs, and his
words fo labour and are fo loaded with heat
and vapour, that, but for laughing, we fhould
pity him; laugh, however, we muft at the
extreme incongruity of a man at once corpulent and old, affociating with youth in an enterprize demanding the utmoft extravagance
of fpirit, and all the wildnefs of activity :
And this it is which makes his complaints fo
truly ridiculous. " *Give me my horfe !*" fays he,
in another fpirit than that of *Richard*; " *Eight*
" *yards of uneven ground*," adds this *Forrefter of*
Diana, this *enterprizing gentleman of the fhade*,
" *is threefcore and ten miles* a-foot *with me*."---
In the heat and agitation of the robbery, out
comes more and more extravagant inftances of
incongruity. Though he is moft probably
older and much fatter than either of the travellers, yet he calls them, *Bacons, Bacon-fed, and*
gorbellied knaves : " *Hang them*, (fays he) *fat chuffs,*
" *they*

" they hate us youth: What! young men, must
" live:—You are grand Jurors, are ye?. We'll jure
" ye, i'faith." But, as yet, we do not fee the
whole length and breadth of him : This is referved for the braggadocio scene. We expect entertainment, but we don't well know of what kind.
Poins, by his prediction, has given us a hint :
But we do not fee or feel *Falstaff* to be a
Coward, much lefs a boafter; without which
even Cowardice is not fufficiently ridiculous ;
and therefore it is, that on the ftage, we find
them always connected. In this uncertainty
on our part, he is, with much artful preparation, produced.—His entrance is delayed to
ftimulate our expectation; and, at laft, to take
off the dullnefs of anticipation, and to add furprize to pleafure, he is called in, as if for
another purpofe of mirth than what we are
furnifhed with : We now behold him, fluc-
tuating with fiction, and labouring with dif-
fembled paffion and chagrin : Too full for
utterance, *Poins* provokes him by a few fim-

K 2   ple

ple words, containing a fine contraſt of af-
·fected eaſe. "*Welcome* Jack, *where haſt thou*
"*been ?*" But when we hear him burſt forth,
"*A plague on all Cowards! Give me a cup of ſack.*
"*Is there no virtue extant !*"—We are at once
in poſſeſſion of the whole man, and are ready
to hug him, guts, lyes and all, as an inex-
hauſtible fund of pleaſantry and humour.
Cowardice, I apprehend, is out of our thought;
it does not, I think, mingle in our mirth.
As to this point, I have preſumed to ſay already, and I repeat it, that we are, in ·my
opinion, the dupes of our own wiſdom, of
ſyſtematic reaſoning, of ſecond thought, and
after reflection. The firſt ſpectators, I believe,
thought of nothing but the laughable ſcrape
which ſo ſingular a character was falling into,
and were delighted to ſee a humourous and unprincipled wit ſo happily taken in his own
inventions, precluded from all rational defence,
and driven to the neceſſity of crying out, af-

ter

ter a few ludicrous evafions, "*No more of that,*
"Hal, *if thou lov'ft me.*"

I do not conceive myfelf obliged to enter
into a confideration of *Falftaff's* lyes concerning the tranfaction at *Gad's-hill.* I have confidered his conduct as independent of thofe
lyes; I have examined the whole of it apart,
and found it free of Cowardice or' fear, except in one inftance, which I have endeavoured to account for and excufe. I have therefore
a right to infer that thofe lyes are to be derived, not from Cowardice, but from fome other
part of his character, which it does not concern me to examine : But I have not content-
ed myfelf hitherto with this fort of negative
defence; and the reader I believe is aware
that I am refolute (though I confefs not un-
tired) to carry this fat rogue out of the reach
of every imputation which affects, or may feem
to affect, his natural Courage.

The

The firſt obſervation then which ſtrikes us, as to his braggadocioes, is, that they are brag-gadocioes *after the faĉt*. In other caſes we ſee the Coward of the Play bluſter and boaſt for a time, talk of diſtant wars, and private duels, out of the reach of knowledge and of evi-dence; of ſtorms and ſtratagems, and of falling in upon the enemy pell-mell and putting thou-ſands to the ſword; till, at length, on the proof of ſome preſent and apparent faĉt, he is brought to open and *laſting* ſhame; to ſhame I mean as a *Coward*; for as to what there is of *lyar* in the caſe, it is conſidered only as acceſſory and ſcarcely reckoned into the ac-count of diſhonour.-- But in the inſtance be-fore us, every thing is reverſed : The Play opens with the *Faĉt*; a Faĉt, from its circum-ſtances as well as from the age and inaĉtivity of the man, very excuſable and capable of much apology, if not of defence. This Faĉt is preceded by no bluſter or pretence what-ever ;—the lies and braggadocioes follow; but

they

they are not *general*; they are confined, and have reference to this one Fact only; the detection is *immediate*; and after fome accompanying mirth and laughter, the fhame of that detection ends; it has no *duration*, as in other cafes; and, for the reft of the Play, the character ftands juft where it did before *without any punifhment or degradation whatever.*

To account for all this, let us only fuppofe that *Falftaff* was a man of natural Courage, though in all refpects unprincipled; but that he was furprized in one fingle inftance into an act of real terror; which, inftead of excufing upon circumftances, he endeavours to cover by lyes and braggadocio; and that thefe lyes become thereupon the fubject, in this place, of detection. Upon thefe fuppofitions the whole difficulty will vanifh at once, and every thing be natural, common, and plain. The *Fact* itfelf will be of courfe *excufable*; that is, it will arife out of a combination of fuch circum-

K 4

ſtances, as being applicable to one caſe only, will not deſtroy the general character : It will not be *preceded* by any braggadocio, containing any fair indication of Cowardice; as real Cowardice is not ſuppoſed to exiſt in the character. But the firſt act of real or apparent Cowardice would naturally throw a vain unprincipled man into the uſe of lyes and braggadocio; but theſe would have reference only to the *Fact in queſtion,* and not apply to other caſes or infect his general character, which is not ſuppoſed to ſtand in need of impoſition. Again,—the detection of Cowardice as ſuch, is more diverting after a long and various courſe of Pretence, where the lye of character is preſerved, as it were, whole, and brought into ſufficient magnitude for a burſt of diſcovery yet, mere occaſional lyes, ſuch as *Falſtaff* is hereby ſuppoſed to utter, are, for the purpoſe of ſport, beſt detected in the telling; becauſe, indeed, they cannot be preſerved for a future time; the exigence and the

humour

humour will be paft: But the *fhame* arifing to *Falftaff* from the detection of *mere lyes* would be *temporary only*; his character as to this point, being already known, and *tolerated for the hu-mour.* Nothing, therefore, could follow but mirth and laughter, and the temporary triumph of baffling a wit at his own weapons, and re-ducing him to an abfolute furrender: After which, we ought not to be furprized if we fee him rife again, like a boy from play, and run another race with as little difhonour as before.

What then can we fay, but that it is clearly the lyes only, not the *Cowardice* of *Falftaff* which are here detected : *Lyes*, to which what there may be of Cowardice is incidental only, improving indeed the Jeft, but by no means the real Bufinefs of the fcene.—And now alfo we may more clearly difcern the true force and meaning of *Poins's* prediction. " *The Jeft* " *will be*, fays he, *the incomprehenfible Lyes that* " *this*

" *this fat rogue will tell us :* How *thirty at*
" *leaft he fought with :*—*and in the reproof of*
" *this lyes the jeft ;*" That is, in the detection
of thefe lyes *fimply* ; for as to *Courage*, he had
never ventured to infinuate more than that
Falftaff would not fight longer than he faw
caufe : *Poins* was in expectation indeed that
Falftaff would fall into fome difhonour on
this occafion ; an event highly probable : But
this was not, it feems, to be the principal
ground of their mirth, but the detection of
thofe *incomprehenfible lyes*, which he boldly
predicts, upon his knowledge of *Falftaff's* character, this *fat rogue*, not *Coward*, would tell
them. This prediction therefore, and the completion of it, go only to the impeachment
of *Falftaff's veracity* and not of his *Courage. Thefe*
" *lyes*, fays the Prince, *are like the father of*
" *them, grofs as a mountain, open, palpable.*—
" *Why thou clay-brained gutts, thou knotty pa-*
" *ted fool ; how couldft thou know thefe men in Ken-*
dal

" *dal Green, when it was so dark thou couldst*
" *not see thy hand ? Come tell us your reason."*

" Poins. *Come your reason,* Jack, *your reason."*

" Again, says the Prince, *Hear how a plain*
" *Tale shall put you down—What trick, what de-*
" *vice, what starting hole canst thou now find*
" *out to hide thee from this open and apparent*
" *shame ?"*

" Poins. *Come let's hear,* Jack, *what trick*
hast thou now ?"

All this clearly refers to *Falstaff's* lyes only
as such; and the objection seems to be, that
he had not told them well, and with sufficient
skill and probability. Indeed nothing seems to
have been required of *Falstaff* at any period
of time but a good evasion. The truth is,
that there is so much mirth, and so little of
malice or imposition, in his fictions, that they
may

may for the moſt part be conſidered as mere
ſtrains of humour and exerciſes of wit, im-
peachable only for defeƈt, when that happens, of the quality from which they are
principally derived. Upon this occaſion *Fal-*
ſtaff's evaſions fail him; he is at the end
of his invention; and it ſeems fair that in
defeƈt of wit, the law ſhould paſs upon him,
and that he ſhould undergo the temporary
cenſure of that Cowardice which he could
not paſs off by any evaſion whatever. The beſt
he could think of, was *inſtinƈt:* He was indeed a *Coward upon inſtinƈt*; in that reſpeƈt *like*
a valiant lion, who would not touch the true Prince.
It would have been a vain attempt, the reader will eaſily perceive, in *Falſtaff,* to have
gone upon other ground, and to have aimed
at juſtifying his Courage by a ſerious vindication: This would have been to have miſtaken
the true point of argument: It was his *lyes,*
not his *Courage,* which was really in queſtion.
There was beſides no getting out of the toils

in

in which he had entangled himfelf: If he was not, he ought at leaſt, by his own ſhewing, to have *been at half-ſword with a dozen of them two hours together*; whereas, it unfortunately appears, and that too evidently to be evaded, that he had run with fingular celerity from *two*, after the exchange of *a few blows* only. This precluded *Falſtaff* from all rational defence in his own perſon;---but it has not precluded me, who am not the advocate of his *lyes* but of his *Courage*.

But there are other fingularities in *Falſtaff's* lyes, which go more directly to his vindication.—That they are confined to one ſcene and one occaſion only, we are not *now* at a loſs to account for;—but what ſhall we ſay to their extravagance? The lyes of *Parolles* and *Bobadill* are brought into ſome ſhape; but the fictions of *Falſtaff* are ſo prepoſterous and *incomprehenſible*, that one may fairly doubt if they ever were intended for credit; and

therefore

therefore, if they ought to be called *lyes*, and not rather *humour*; or, to compound the matter, *humourous rhodomontades*. Certain it is, that they deſtroy their own purpoſe and are clearly not the effect, in this reſpect, of a regulated practice, and habit of impoſition. The real truth ſeems to be, that had *Falſtaff*, looſe and unprincipled as he is, been born a Coward and bred a Soldier, he muſt, naturally, have been a great *Braggadocio*, a true *miles glorioſus :* But in ſuch caſe he ſhould have been exhibited active and young; for it is plain, that age and corpulency are an excuſe for Cowardice, which ought not to be afforded him. In the preſent caſe, wherein he was not only involved in ſuſpicious circumſtances, but wherein he ſeems to have felt ſome conſcious touch of infirmity, and having no candid conſtruction to expect from his laughing companions, he burſts at once, and with all his might, into the moſt unweighed and preposterous fictions, determined to put to proof

on

on this occafion his boafted talent of *fwearing truth out of England.* He tried it here, to its utmoft extent, and was unfortunately routed on his own ground; which indeed, with fuch a mine beneath his feet, could not be other-wife. But without this, he had mingled in his deceits fo much whimfical humour and fantaftic exaggeration that he muft have been detected; and herein appears the admirable addrefs of *Shakefpeare,* who can fhew us *Fal-ftaff* in the various light, not only of what he is, but what he would have been under one fingle variation of character,—the want of natural Courage; whilft with an art not enough underftood, he moft effectually preferves the real character of *Falftaff* even in the moment he feems to depart from it, by making his lyes too extravagant for practifed impofition; by grounding them more upon humour than deceit; and turning them, as we fhall next fee, into a fair and honeft proof of general Cou-rage, by appropriating them to the conceal-

ment

ment only of a fingle exception. And hence
it is, that we fee him draw fo deeply and
fo confidently upon his former credit for Courage and atchievment : *" I never dealt better in*
" my life,—thou know'ſt my old ward, Hal;" are expreſſions, which clearly refer to fome known
feats and defences of his former life. His
exclamations   againſt Cowardice, his reference to his own manhood, *" Die when*
" thou wilt old Jack, *if manhood, good man-*
" hood, be not forgot upon the face of the earth,
" then am I a ſhotten herring :"   Thefe, and
various expreſſions ſuch as thefe, would be
abfurdities not impofitions, Farce not Comedy,
if not calculated to conceal fome defect fuppofed unknown to the hearers ; and thefe hearers were, in the prefent cafe, his conſtant
companions, and the daily witneſſes of his conduct.   If before this period he had been a
known and detected Coward, and was confcious that he had no credit to lofe, I fee no
reafon why he ſhould fly fo violently from a

familiar

familiar ignominy which had often before attached him; or why falſhoods, ſeemingly in
ſuch a caſe, neither calculated for or expecting
credit, ſhould be cenſured, or detected, as lyes
or impoſition.

That the whole tranſaction was conſidered
as a mere jeſt, and as carrying with it no ſerious imputation on the Courage of *Falſtaff* is
manifeſt, not only from his being allowed,
when the laugh was paſt, to call himſelf,
without contradiction in the perſonated character of *Hal* himſelf, " valiant *Jack Falſtaff, and*
" *the more* valiant *being, as he is,* old Jack Falſtaff,"
but from various other particulars, and, above
all, from the declaration, which the Prince
makes on that very night of his intention of
procuring this *fat rogue a Charge of foot;*—a
circumſtance, doubtleſs, contrived by *Shakeſpeare*
to wipe off the ſeeming diſhonour of the day:
And from this time forward, we hear of no
imputation ariſing from this tranſaction; it is

L   born

born and dies in a convivial hour; it leaves
no trace behind, nor do we fee any longer
in the character of *Falftaff* the boafting or
braggadocio of a Coward.

Tho' I have confidered *Falftaff*'s character
as relative only to one fingle quality, yet fo
much has been faid, that it cannot efcape the
reader's notice that he is a character made up
by *Shakefpeare* wholly of incongruities ;---a man
at once young and old, enterprizing and fat,
a dupe and a wit, harmlefs and wicked, weak
in principle and refolute by conftitution, cowardly in appearance and brave in reality ; a
knave without malice, a lyar without deceit ;
and a knight, a gentleman, and a foldier, without either dignity, decency, or honour: This
is a character, which, though it may be de-
compounded, could not, I believe, have been
formed, nor the ingredients of it duly mingled
upon any receipt whatever: It required the
hand of *Shakefpeare* himfelf to give to every

particular

particular part a relifh of the whole, and of the whole to every particular part;---alike the fame incongruous, identical *Falftaff*, whether to the grave Chief Juftice he vainly talks of his youth, and offers to *caper for a thoufand*; or cries to Mrs. *Doll*, " *I am old, I am old,*" though fhe is feated on his lap, and he is courting her for buffes. How *Shakefpeare* could furnifh out fentiment of fo extraordinary a compofition, and fupply it with fuch appropriated and characteriftic language, humour and wit, I cannot tell; but I may, however, venture to infer, and that confidently, that he who fo well underftood the ufes of incongruity, and that laughter was to be raifed by the oppofition of qualities in the fame man, and not by their agreement or conformity, would never have attempted to raife mirth by fhewing us Cowardice in a Coward unattended by Pretence, and foftened by every excufe of age, corpulence, and infirmity: And of this we cannot have a more ftriking proof than his furnifh-

L 2   ing

ing this very character, on one inftance of real terror, however excufable, with boaft, braggadocio, and pretence, exceeding that of all other ftage Cowards the whole length of his fuperior wit, humour, and invention.

What then upon the whole fhall be faid but that *Shakefpeare* has made certain Impreffions, or produced certain effects, of which he has thought fit to conceal or obfcure the caufe? How he has done this, and for what fpecial ends, we fhall now prefume to guefs.--- Before the period in which *Shakefpeare* wrote, the fools and Zanys of the ftage were drawn out of the coarfeft and cheapeft materials : Some effential folly, with a dafh of knave and coxcomb, did the feat. But *Shakefpeare*, who delighted in difficulties, was refolved to furnifh a richer repaft, and to give to one eminent buffoon the high relifh of wit, humour, birth, dignity, and Courage. But this was a procefs which required the niceft hand, and the utmoft moſt management and addreſs: Theſe enumerated qualities are, in their own nature, productive of *reſpect*; an Impreſſion the moſt oppoſite to laughter that can be. This Impreſſion then, it was, at all adventures, neceſſary to with-hold; which could not perhaps well be without dreſſing up theſe qualities in fantaſtic forms, and colours not their own; and thereby cheating the eye with ſhews of baſeneſs and of folly, whilſt he ſtole as it were upon the palate a richer and a fuller *goût*. To this end, what arts, what contrivances, has he not practiſed! How has he ſteeped this ſingular character in bad habits for fifty years together, and brought him forth ſaturated with every folly and with every vice not deſtructive of his eſſential character, or incompatible with his own primary deſign! For this end, he has deprived *Falſtaff* of every good principle; and for another, which will be preſently mentioned, he has concealed every bad one. He has given him alſo every infirmity of body

that

that is not likely to awaken our compaffion, and which is moft proper to render both his better qualities and his vices ridiculous; He has affociated levity and debauch with *age*, corpulence and inactivity with *courage*, and has roguifhly coupled the gout with *Military honours*, and a *penfion* with the *pox*. He has likewife involved this character in fituations, out of which neither wit or Courage can extricate him with honour. The furprize at *Gads-hill* might have betrayed a hero into flight, and the encounter with *Douglas* left him no choice but death or ftratagem. If he plays an after-game, and endeavours to redeem his ill fortune by lies and braggadocio, his ground fails him; no wit, no evafion will avail: Or is he likely to appear refpectable in his perfon, rank, and demeanor, how is that refpect abated or difcharged! *Shakefpeare* has given him a kind of ftate indeed; but of what is it compofed? Of that fuftian cowardly rafcal *Piftol*, and his yoke-fellow of few words the

equally

equally deedlefs *Nym*; of his cup-bearer the
fiery *Trigon*, whofe zeal burns in his nofe,
Bardolph; and of the boy, who bears the purfe
with *feven groats and two-pence*;—a boy who was
given him on purpofe to fet him off, and
whom he walks *before*, according to his own
defcription, " *like a fow that had overwhelmed*
" *all her litter but one.*"

But it was not enough to render *Falftaff* ridiculous in his figure, fituations, and equi-
page ; *ftill* his refpectable qualities would have
come forth, at leaft occafionally, to fpoil our
mirth ; or they might have burft the inter-
vention of fuch flight impediments, and have
every where fhone through : It was neceffary
then to go farther, and throw on him that fubftantial ridicule, which only the incongruities
of real vice can furnifh ; of vice, which was
to be fo mixed and blended with his frame
as to give a durable character and colour to
the whole,

L 4

But

But it may here be neceſſary to detain the reader a moment in order to apprize him of my further intention; without which, I might hazard that good underſtanding, which I hope has hitherto been preſerved between us.

I have 'till now looked only to the Courage of *Falſtaff*, a quality which having been denied, in terms, to belong to his conſtitution, I have endeavoured to vindicate to the Underſtandings of my readers; the Impreſſion on their Feelings (in which all Dramatic-truth conſiſts) being already, as I have ſuppoſed, in favour of the character. In the purſuit of this ſubject I have taken the general Impreſſion of the whole character pretty much, I ſuppoſe, like other men; and, when occaſion has required, have ſo tranſmitted it to the reader; joining in the common Feeling of *Falſtaff*'s pleaſantry, his apparent freedom from ill principle, and his companionable wit and good humour: With a ſtage character, in the article

cle of exhibition, we have nothing more to
do; for in fact what is it but an Impreffion;
an appearance, which we are to confider as a
reality; and which we may venture to applaud or condemn as fuch, without further inquiry or inveftigation? But if we would account for our Impreffions, or for certain fentiments or actions in a character, not derived
from its apparent principles, yet appearing, we
know not why, natural, we are then compelled
to look farther, and examine if there be not
fomething more in the character than is
fhewn; fomething inferred, which is not brought
under our fpecial notice: In fhort, we muft
look to the art of the writer, and to the principles of human nature, to difcover the hidden caufes of fuch effects.—Now this is a
very different matter—The former confidera-
tions refpected the Impreffion only, without
regard to the Underftanding; but this queftion
relates to the Underftanding alone. It is true
that there are but few Dramatic characters
which

which will bear this kind of inveftigation, as
not being drawn in exact conformity to thofe
principles of general nature to which we muft
refer. But this is not the cafe with regard to
the characters of *Shakefpeare*; they are ftruck
out *whole*, by fome happy art which I cannot
clearly comprehend, out of the general mafs of
things, from the block as it were of nature:
And it is, I think, an eafier thing to give a
juft draught of man from thefe Theatric forms,
which I cannot help confidering as originals,
than by drawing from real life, amidft fo
much intricacy, obliquity, and difguife. If
therefore, for further proofs of *Falftaff's* Courage, or for the fake of curious fpeculation,
or for both, I change my pofition, and look
to caufes inftead of effects, the reader muft
not be furprized if he finds the former *Falftaff*
vanifh like a dream, and another, of more dif-
guftful form, prefented to his view; one, whofe
final punifhment we fhall be fo far from re-
gretting, that we ourfelves fhall be ready to
confign him to a feverer doom.

The

The reader will very eafily apprehend that a character, which we might wholly difap-prove of, confidered as exifting in human life, may yet be thrown on the ftage into certain peculiar fituations, and be compreffed by ex-ternal influences into fuch temporary appear-ances, as may render fuch character for a time highly acceptable and entertaining, and even more diftinguifhed for qualities, which on this fuppofition would be accidents only, than an-other character really poffeffing thofe qualities, but which, under the preffure of the fame fi-tuation and influences, would be diftorted into a different form, or totally loft in timidity and weaknefs. If therefore the character before us will admit of this kind of inveftigation, our Inquiry will not be without fome dignity, confidered as extending to the principles of human nature, and to the genius and arts of Him, who has beft caught every various form of the human mind, and tranfmitted them with the greateft happinefs and fidelity.

To

To return then to the vices of *Falſtaff.*---
We have frequently referred to them under
the name of ill habits;---but perhaps the reader is not fully aware how very vicious he indeed is;---he is a robber, a glutton, a cheat,
a drunkard, and a lyar; laſcivious, vain, info-
lent, profligate, and profane:---A fine infuſion
this, and ſuch as without very excellent cook-
ery muſt have thrown into the diſh a great
deal too much of the *fumet.* It was a nice operation;---theſe vices were not only to be of a
particular ſort, but it was alſo neceſſary to
guard them at both ends; on the *one*, from
all appearance of malicious motive, and indeed
from the manifeſtation of any ill principle
whatever, which muſt have produced *diſguſt*,---
a ſenſation no leſs oppoſite to laughter than is
reſpeEt;---and, on the *other*, from the notice, or
even apprehenſion, in the ſpeEtators, of *pernicious*
effeEt; which produces *grief* and *terror*, and is
the proper province of Tragedy alone.

Actions cannot with ftrict propriety be faid to be either virtuous or vicious: Thefe quali-ties, or attributes, belong to *agents* only ; and are derived, even in refpect to *them,* from in-tention alone. The abftracting of qualities, and confidering them as independent of any *fubject,* and the applying of them afterwards to actions independent of the agent, is a dou-ble operation which I do not pretend, thro' any part of it, to underftand. All actions may moft properly, in their own nature, I think, be called *neutral;* tho' in common dif-courfe, and in writing where precifion is not requifite, we often term them *vicious,* tranf-fering on thefe occafions the attributive from the *agent* to the *action* ; and fometimes we call them *evil,* or of pernicious effect, by tranf-ferring, in like manner, the injuries inciden-tally arifing from certain actions to the life, happinefs, or intereft of human beings, to the natural operation, whether moral or phyfical, of the *actions* themfelves : *One* is a colour
thrown

thrown on them by the *intention*, in which I
think confifts all moral turpitude, and the
other by effect: If therefore a Dramatic
writer will ufe certain managements to keep
vicious intention as much as poffible from
our notice, and make us fenfible that no
evil effect follows, he may pafs off actions
of very vicious motive, without much ill impreffion, as mere *incongruities*, and the effect
of *humour* only;—*words thefe*, which, as applied to human conduct, are employed, I believe, to cover a great deal of what may deferve much harder appellation.

The *difference* between fuffering an evil effect to take place, and of preventing fuch
effect, from actions precifely of the fame nature, is fo great, that it is often *all the difference* between Tragedy and Comedy. The Fine
gentleman of the Comic fcene, who fo
promptly draws his fword, and wounds, without killing, fome other gentleman of the
fame

fame fort; and *He* of Tragedy, whofe ftabs
are mortal, differ very frequently in no other
point whatever. If our *Falftaff* had really
peppered (as he calls it) *two rogues in buckram
fuits*, we muft have looked for a very different
conclufion, and have expected to have found
Falftaff's Effential profe converted into blank
verfe, and to have feen him move off, in
flow and meafured paces, like the City Pren-
tice to the tolling of a Paffing bell;—*" he
" would have become a cart as well as another,
" or a plague on his bringing up."*

Every incongruity in a rational being is a
fource of laughter, whether it refpects manners, fentiments, conduct, or even drefs, or fituation ;—but the greateft of all poffible incongruity is vice, whether in the intention itfelf, or as transferred to, and becoming more
manifeft in action ;—it is inconfiftent with moral
agency, nay, with rationality itfelf, and all the
ends and purpofes of our being.—Our author
defcribes

defcribes the natural ridicule of vice in his
MEASURE *for* MEASURE in the ftrongeft
terms, where, after having made the angels
weep over the vices of men, he adds, that
with our fpleens *they might laugh themfelves quite
mortal.* Indeed if we had a perfect difcernment
of the ends of this life only, and could
preferve ourfelves from fympathy, difguft and
terror, the vices of mankind would be a
fource of ·perpetual entertainment. The great
difference between *Heraclitus* and *Democritus* lay,
it feems, in their fpleen only ;—for a wife and
good man muft either laugh or cry without
ceafing. Nor indeed is it eafy to conceive
(to inftance in one cafe only) a more
laughable, or a more melancholy object, than
a human being, his nature and duration confidered, earneftly and anxioufly exchanging
peace of mind and confcious integrity for
gold ; and for gold too, which he has often
no occafion for, or dares not employ :—But

Voltaire

Voltaire has by one Publication rendered all *arguments* fuperfluous : He has told us, in his *Candide,* the merrieft and moft diverting tale of frauds, murders, maffacres, rapes, rapine, de-folation, and deftruction, that I think it pof-fible on any other plan to invent; and he has given us *motive* and *effect,* with every pof-fible aggravation, to improve the fport. One would think it difficult to preferve the point of ridicule, in fuch a cafe, unabated by contrary emotions ; but now that the feat is performed it appears of eafy imitation, and I am amazed that our race of imitators have made no efforts in this fort: It would anfwer I fhould think in the way of profit, not to mention the moral ufes to which it might be applied. The managements of *Voltaire* confift in this, that he affumes a gay, eafy, and light tone himfelf; that he never ex-cites the reflections of his readers by making any of his own; that he hurries us on with fuch a rapidity of narration as prevents our

M

emotions

emotions from refting on any particular point;
and to gain this end, he has intervoven the
conclufion of one fact fo into the commencement of another, that we find ourfelves engaged in new matter before we are fenfible
that we had finifhed the old; he has likewife made his crimes fo enormous, that we
do not fadden on any fympathy, or find
ourfelves partakers in the guilt.—But what is
truly fingular as to this book, is, that it
does not appear to have been written for any
moral purpofe, but for That only (if I do
not err) of fatyrifing Providence itfelf; a defign fo enormoufly profane, that it may well
pafs for the moft ridiculous part of the
whole compofition.

But if vice, divefted of difguft and terror,
is thus in its own nature ridiculous, we ought
not to be furprifed if the very fame vices
which fpread horror and defolation thro' the
Tragic fcene fhould yet furnifh the Comic
with

with its higheſt. laughter and delight, and that
tears, and mirth, and even humour and wit
itſelf, ſhould grow from the ſame root of
incongruity: For what is humour in the hu-
mouriſt, bur incongruity, whether of ſentiment,
conduct, or manners? What in the man of
humour, but a quick diſcernment, and keen
ſenſibility of theſe incongruities? And what is
wit itſelf, without preſuming however to give
a complete definition where ſo many have
failed, but a talent, for the moſt part, of
marking with force and vicacity unexpected
points of likeneſs in things ſuppoſed incongruous, and points of incongruity in things ſuppoſed alike: And hence it is that wit and humour,
tho' always diſtinguiſhed, are ſo often coupled
together; it being very poſſible, I ſuppoſe, to
be a man of humour without wit; but I
think not a man of wit without humour.

But I have here raiſed ſo much new matter,
that the reader may be out of hope of ſee-

ing

ing this argument, any more than the tale of
Triſtram, brought to a concluſion: He may
ſuppoſe me now prepared to turn my pen to
a moral, or to a dramatic Eſſay, or ready to
draw the line between vice and virtue, or
Comedy and Tragedy, as fancy ſhall lead the
way;---But he is happily miſtaken; I am pref-
ſing earneſtly, and not without ſome impati-
ence, to a concluſion. The principles I have
now opened are neceſſary to be conſidered for
the purpoſe of eſtimating the character of *Falſtaff*, conſidered as relatively to human nature: I
ſhall then reduce him with all poſſible dif-
patch to his Theatric condition, and reſtore
him, I hope, without injury, to the ſtage.

There is indeed a vein or two of argument
running through the matter that now ſurrounds
me, which I might open for my own more
peculiar purpoſes; but which, having refiſted
much greater temptations, I ſhall wholly de-
ſert. It ought not, however, to be forgotten,
that

that if *Shakefpeare* has ufed arts to abate our refpect of *Falftaff*, it fhould follow by juft inference, that, without fuch arts, his character would have grown into a *refpect* inconfiftent with laughter; and that yet, without Courage, he could not have been refpectable at all;---that it required nothing lefs than the union of ability and Courage to fupport his other more accidental qualities with any tolerable coherence. Courage and Ability are firft principles of Character, and not to be deftroyed whilft the united frame of body and mind continues whole and unimpaired; they are the pillars on which he ftands firm in fpight of all his vices and difgraces;---but if we fhould take Courage away, and reckon Cowardice among his other defects, all the intelligence and wit in the world could not fupport him through a fingle Play.

The effect of taking away the influence of this quality upon the manners of a character,

racter, tho' the quality and the influence be affumed only, is evident in the cafes of *Parolles*
and *Bobadil*. *Parolles*, at leaft, did not feem
to want wit; but both thefe characters are reduced almoft to non-entity, and after their
difgraces, walk only thro' a fcene or two, the
mere mockery of their former exiftence. *Parolles*
was fo changed, that neither the *fool*, nor the
old lord *Le-feu*, could readily recollect his
perfon; and his wit feemed to be annihilated
with his Courage.

Let it not be here objected that *Falftaff* is
univerfally confidered as a Coward;—we do
indeed call him fo; but that is nothing,
if the character itfelf does not act from any
confcioufnefs of this kind, and if our Feelings take his part, and revolt againft our
underftanding,

As to the arts by which *Shakefpeare* has
contrived to obfcure the vices of *Falftaff*, they
are

fuch, as being fubfervient only to the mirth
of the Play, I do not feel myfelf obliged to
detail.

But it may be well worth our curiofity to
inquire into the compofition of *Falftaff*'s character.—Every man we may obferve, has two
characters; that is, every man may be feen
externally, and from without ;—or a fection
may be made of him, and he may be illumi-
nated from within.

Of the external character of *Falftaff*, we
can fcarcely be faid to have any fteady view.
Jack Falftaff we are familiar with, but *Sir John*
was better known, it feems, *to the reft of Europe,*
than to his intimate companions; yet we have
fo many glimpfes of him, and he is opened
to us occafionally in fuch various points of
view, that we cannot be miftaken in defcrib-
ing him as a man of birth and fafhion, bred
up in all the learning and accomplifhments of
the

the times ;—of ability and Courage equal to any
fituation, and capable by nature of the higheſt
affairs ; trained to arms, and poſſeſſing the
tone, the deportment, and the manners of a
gentleman ;—but yet theſe accompliſhments and
advantages feem to hang loofe on him, and
to be worn with a ſlovenly careleſſneſs and in-
attention : A too great indulgence of the qualities of humour and wit feems to draw him
too much one way, and to deſtroy the grace
and orderly arrangement of his other accompliſhments ;—and hence he becomes ſtrongly
marked for one advantage, to the injury, and
almoſt forgetfulneſs in the beholder, of all the
reſt. Some of his vices likewife ſtrike through,
and ſtain his Exterior ;—his modes of fpeech
betray a certain licentiouſneſs of mind ; and
that high Ariſtrocratic tone which belonged to his fituation was puſhed on, and
aggravated into unfeeling infolence and oppreſ-
fion. *" It is not a confirmed brow,"* ſays the Chief
Juſtice,

Juſtice, *"nor the throng of words that come with* *" ſuch more than impudent ſaucineſs from you, can* *" thruſt me from a level conſideration :"* *" My lord,* anſwers *Falſtaff,* *" you call honourable boldneſs im-* *" pudent ſaucineſs.* *If a man will court'ſie and ſay* *" nothing, he is virtuous :* No *my lord, my humble* *" duty remembered, I will not be your ſuitor. I ſay* *" to you I deſire deliverance from theſe officers, being* *" upon haſty employment in the King's affairs."* *" You ſpeak,* replies the Chief Juſtice, *" as hav-* *" ing power to do wrong."*—His whole behaviour to the Chief Juſtice, whom he deſpairs of winning by flattery, is ſingularly inſolent; and the reader will remember many inſtances of his inſolence to others : Nor are his manners always free from the taint of vulgar ſociety; —*"This is the right fencing grace, my lord,"* (ſays he to the Chief Juſtice, with great impropriety of manners) *" tap for tap, and ſo part fair :"* *" Now* *" the lord lighten thee,"* is the reflection of the Chief Juſtice, *" thou art a very great fool."*—

Such

Such a character as I have here defcribed, ftrengthened with that vigour, force, and alacrity of mind, of which he is poffeffed, muft have fpread terror and difmay thro' the ignorant, the timid, the modeft, and the weak : Yet is he however, when occafion requires, capable of much accomodation and flattery ;—and in order to obtain the protection and patronage of the great, fo convenient to his vices and his po-verty, he was put under the daily neceffity of practifing and improving thefe arts ; a bafe-nefs, which he compenfates to himfelf, like other unprincipled men, by an increafe of in-folence towards his inferiors.—There is alfo a natural activity about *Falftaff*, which for want of proper employment, fhews itfelf in a kind of fwell or buftle, which feems to cor-refpond with his bulk, as if his mind had inflated his body, and demanded a habitation of no lefs circumference : Thus conditioned he rolls (in the language of *Offian*) like a *Whale of Ocean*, fcattering the fmaller fry ; but afford-

ing

ing, in his turn, noble contention to *Hal* and *Poins*; who, to keep up the allufion, I may be allowed on this occafion to compare 'to the Threfher and the Sword-fifh.

To this part of *Falftaff's* character, many things which he does and fays, and which appear unaccountably natural, are to be referred.

We are next to fee him *from within*: And here we fhall behold him moft villainoufly unprincipled and debauched; poffeffing indeed the fame Courage and ability, yet ftained with numerous vices, unfuited not only to his primary qualities, but to his age, corpulency, rank, and profeffion;---reduced by thefe vices to a ftate of dependence, yet refolutely bent to indulge them at any price. Thefe vices have been already enumerated; they are many, and become ftill more intolerable by an ex-

cefs

cefs of unfeeling infolence on one hand, and of bafe accomodation on the other.

But what then, after all, is become of *old Jack* ? Is this the jovial delightful companion ;-- *Falftaff*, the favourite and the boaft of the Stage ?---by no means. But it is, I think however, the *Falftaff* of Nature ; the very ftuff out of which the *Stage Falftaff* is compofed ; nor was it poffible, I believe, out of of any other materials he could have been formed. From this difagreable draught we fhall be able, I truft, by a proper difpofition of light and fhade, and from the influence and compreffion of external things, to produce *plump Jack*, the life of humour, the fpirit of pleafantry, and the foul of mirth.

To this end, *Falftaff* muft no longer be confidered as a fingle independent character, but grouped, as we find him fhewn to us in the Play ;—his ability muft be difgraced by buffoonery,

buffoonery, and his Courage by circumſtances of imputation; and thoſe qualities be thereupon reduced into ſubjeƈts of mirth and laughter :— His vices muſt be concealed at each end from vicious deſign and evil effeƈt, and muſt there-upon be turned into incongruities, and aſſume the name of humour only ;—his inſolence muſt be repreſſed by the ſuperior tone of *Hal* and *Poins,* and take the ſofter name of ſpirit only, or alacrity of mind ;—his ſtate of depend-ence, his temper of accomodation, and his aƈti-vity, muſt fall in preciſely with the indul-gence of his humours; that is, he muſt thrive beſt and flatter moſt, by being extravagantly incongruous; and his own tendency, impelled by ſo much aƈtivity, will carry him with perfeƈt eaſe and freedom to all the neceſſary exceſſes. But why, it may be aſked, ſhould incongruities recommend *Falſtaff* to the favour of the Prince?—Becauſe the Prince is ſup-poſed to poſſeſs a high reliſh of humour and

and to have a temper and a force about him,
which, whatever was his purfuit, delighted
in excefs. This, *Falftaff* is fuppofed perfectly
to comprehend ; and thereupon not only to
indulge himfelf in all kinds of incongruity,
but to lend out his own fuperior wit and
humour againft himfelf, and to heighten the
ridicule by all the tricks and arts of buffoonery for which his corpulence, his age,
and fituation, furnifh fuch excellent materials.
This compleats the Dramatic character of
Falftaff, and gives him that appearance of
perfect good-nature, pleafantry, mellownefs,
and hilarity of mind, for which we admire
and almoft love him, tho' we feel certain re-
ferves which forbid our going that length;
the true reafon of which is, that there will
be always found a difference between mere
appearances, and reality : Nor are we, nor can
we be, infenfible that whenever the action of
external influence upon him is in whole
or in part relaxed, the character reftores

itfelf

itfelf proportionably to its more unpleafing condition.

A character really poffeffing the quailties which are on the, ftage imputed to *Falftaff*, would be beft fhewn by its own natural ener-gy; the leaft compreffion would diforder it, and make us feel for it all the pain of fym-pathy: It is the artificial condition of *Falftaff* which is the fource of our delight; we enjoy his diftreffes, we *gird at him* ourfelves, and urge the fport without the leaft alloy of compaffion; and we give him, when the laugh is over, undeferved credit for the pleafure we enjoyed. If any one thinks that thefe obfervations are the effect of too much refinement, and that there was in truth more of chance in the cafe than of management or defign, let him try his own luck;—perhaps he may draw out of the wheel of fortune a *Macbeth*, an *Othello*, a *Benedict*, or a *Falftaff*.

Such

Such, I think, is the true character of this extraordinary buffoon; and from hence we may difcern for what fpecial purpofes *Shakefpeare* has given him talents and qualities, which were to be afterwards obfcured, and perverted to ends oppofite to their nature; it was clearly to furnifh out a Stage buffoon of a peculiar fort; a kind of Game-bull which would ftand the baiting thro' a hundred Plays, and produce equal fport, whether he is pinned down occafionally by *Hal* or *Poins*, or toffes fuch mongrils as *Bardolph*, or the Juftices, fprawling in the air. There is in truth no fuch thing as totally demolifhing *Falftaff*; he has fo much of the invulnerable in his frame that no ridicule can deftroy him; he is fafe even in defeat, and feems to rife, like another *Antæus*, with recruited vigour from every fall; in this as in every other refpéct, unlike *Parolles* or *Bobadil*: They fall by the firft fhaft of ridicule, but *Falftaff* is a butt on which we may empty the whole quiver, whilft the

fubftance

fubftance of his character remains unimpaired. His ill habits, and the accidents of age and corpulence, are no part of his effential con-ftitution ; they come forward indeed on our eye, and folicit our notice, but they are fecond natures, not *firft*; mere fhadows, we purfue them in vain; *Falftaff* himfelf has a diftinct and feparate fubfiftence; he laughs at the chace, and when the fport is over, gathers them with unruffled feather under his wing : And hence it is that he is made to undergo not one detection only, but a feries of detections; that he is not formed for one Play only, but was intended originally at leaft for two; and the author we are told, was doubtful if he fhould not extend him yet farther, and engage him in the wars with *France*. This he might well have done, for there is nothing perifhable in the nature of *Falftaff* : .He might have involved him, by the vicious part of his character, in new difficul-ties and unlucky fituations, and have enabled

N   him

him, by the better part, to have fcrambled
through, abiding and retorting the jefts and
laughter of every beholder.

But whatever we may be told concerning
the intention of *Shakefpeare* to extend this character farther, there is a manifeft preparation
near the end of the fecond part of Henry
IV. for his difgrace : The difguife is taken off,
and he begins openly to pander to the exceffes of the Prince, intitling himfelf to the
character afterwards given him of being *the*
tutor and the feeder of his riots. " *I will fetch*
" *off*," (fays he) " *thefe Juftices.—I will devife*
" *matter enough out of this* Shallow *to keep the Prince*
" *in continual laughter the wearing out of fix*
" *fafhions.—If the young* dace *be a bait for the*
" *old* pike," (fpeaking with reference to his
own defigns upon *Shallow*) " *I fee no reafon in*
" *the law of nature but I may fnap at· him.*"---
This is fhewing himfelf abominably diffolute :
The laborious arts of fraud, which he prac-
tices

tices on *Shallow* to induce the loan of a thoufand pound, create *difguft*; and the more,
as we are fenfible this money was never likely
to be *paid back*, as we are told that *was*, of
which the travellers had been robbed. It is
true we feel no pain for *Shallow*, he being a
very bad character, as would fully appear,
if he were unfolded; but *Falftaff*'s deliberation
in fraud is not on that account more excufable.—The event of the old King's death
draws him out almoft into deteftation.---" *Maf-*
" *ter* Robert Shallow, *chufe what office thou wilt*
" *in the land,*---'*tis thine.*---*I am fortune's fteward.*---
" *let us take any man's horfes.*---*The laws of Eng-*
" *land are at my commandment.*---*Happy are they*
" *who have been my friends;*---*and woe to my*
" Lord Chief Juftice."---After this we ought not
to complain if we fee Poetic juftice duly ex-
ecuted upon him, and that he is finally given
up to fhame and difhonour.

But

But it is remarkable that, during this procefs, we are not acquainted with the fuccefs
of *Falftaff's* defigns upon *Shallow* 'till the moment of his difgrace. " *If I had had time,*" (fays
he to *Shallow*, as the King is approaching,)
" *to have made new liveries, I would have beftowed*
" *the thoufand pounds I borrowed of you ;*"---and
the firft word he utters after this period is,
" *Mafter* Shallow, *I owe you a thoufand pounds :*"
We may from hence very reafonably pre-
fume, that *Shakefpeare* meant to connect this
fraud with the punifhment of *Falftaff*, as a
more avowed ground of cenfure and difhonour : Nor ought the confideration that this
paffage contains the moft exquifite comic humour and propriety in another view, to diminifh the truth of this obfervation.

But however juft it might be to demolifh
Falftaff in this way, by opening to us his
bad principles, it was by no means *convenient.*
If we had been to have feen a fingle reprefentation

fentation of him only, it might have been proper enough; but as he was to be fhewn from night to night, and from age to age, the difguft arifing from the *clofe*, would by degrees have fpread itfelf over the whole character; reference would be had throughout to his bad principles, and he would have become lefs acceptable as he was more known: And yet it was neceffary to bring him, like all other ftage characters, to fome conclufion. Every play muft be wound up by fome event, which may fhut in the characters and the action. If fome *hero* obtains a crown, or a miftrefs, involving therein the fortune of others, we are fatisfied;—we do not defire to be afterwards admitted of his council, or his bedchamber: Or if through jealoufy, caufelefs or well founded, *another* kills a beloved wife, and himfelf after,—there is no more to be faid;—they are dead, and there an end; Or if in the fcenes of Comedy, parties are engaged, and plots formed, for the furthering

or

or preventing the completion of that great article Cuckoldom, we expect to be satisfied in the point as far as the nature of so nice a case will permit, or at least to see such a manifest *disposition* as will leave us in no doubt of the event. By the bye, I cannot but think that the Comic writers of the last age treated this matter as of more importance, and made more bustle about it, than the temper of the present times will well bear; and it is therefore to be hoped that the Dramatic authors of the present day, some of whom, to the best of my judgment, are deserving of great praise, will consider and treat this business, rather as a common and natural incident arising out of modern manners, than as worthy to be held forth as the great object and sole end of the Play.

But whatever be the question, or whatever the character, the curtain must not only be dropt before

before the eyes, but over the minds of the fpectators, and nothing left for further examination and curiofity.—But how was this to be
done in regard to *Falftaff?* He was not involved in the fortune of the Play; he was engaged in no action which, as to him, was to
be compleated; he had reference to no fyftem,
he was attracted to no center; he paffes thro'
the Play as a lawlefs meteor, and we wifh to
know what courfe he is afterwards likely to
take: He is detected and difgraced, it is
true; but he lives by detection, and thrives
on difgrace; and we are defirous to fee him
detected and difgraced again. The *Fleet* might
be no bad fcene of further amufement;—he.
carries *all* within him, *and what matter* where,
if he be ftill the fame, poffeffing the fame force·
of mind, the fame wit, and the fame incongruity. This, *Shakefpeare* was fully fenfible of,
and knew that this character could not be
compleatly difmiffed but by death.—" Our
" author, (fays the Epilogue to the Second
" Part

" Part of Henry IV.) will continue the ſtory
" with Sir *John* in it, and make you merry
" with fair *Catherine* of *France*; where, for any
" thing I know, *Falſtaff* ſhall dye of a ſweat,
" unleſs already he be killed with your hard
" opinions." If it had been prudent in
Shakeſpeare to have killed *Falſtaff* with *hard opi-*
nion, he had the means in his hand to effect
it;---but dye, it ſeems, he muſt, in one form
or another, and a *ſweat* would have been no un-
ſuitable cataſtrophe. However we have reaſon
to be ſatisfied as it is;---his death was worthy
of his birth and of his life: " *He was born,*
he ſays, " *about three o'clock in the afternoon with*
a white head, and ſomething a round belly."
But if he came into the world in the even-
ing with theſe marks of age, he departs
out of it in the morning in all the follies
and vanities of youth;----" *He was ſhaked* (we
" are told) "*of a burning quotidian tertian;---*
' *the young King had run bad humours on the*
" *knight;---his heart was fraEted and corroborate ;*
" *and*

" *and a' parted juft between twelve and one, even*
" *at the turning of the tide, yielding the crow a*
" *pudding, and paffing directly into* Arthur's bofom,
." *if ever man went into the bofom of* Arthur."—
So ended this fingular buffoon; and with him
ends an Effay, on which the reader is left
to beftow what character he pleafes : An Effay
profeffing to treat of the Courage of *Falftaff*,
but extending itfelf to his Whole character;
to the arts and genius of his Poetic-Maker,
SHAKESPEARE; and thro' him fometimes, with
ambitious aim, even to the principles of human nature itfelf.

T H E   E N D.